His Grandfather's House

A Novel By

Ron Fritsch

Copyright © 2017 Ron Fritsch

ISBN: 9780997882933

Published by Asymmetric Worlds

For information, address:

Asymmetric Worlds
1657 West Winona Street
Chicago, IL 60640-2707

http://www.hisgrandfathershouse.com

For David, Lee Ann and my family

List of Characters: The Reinharts

Arny, Kurt's uncle, Johnny's brother, Henry and Bertha's older son, Elaine's husband

Bertha, Kurt's grandmother, Henry's wife, Johnny and Arny's mother

Conrad, Henry's older half brother, Otto's son

Cora, Henry's older half sister, Otto's daughter

Elaine, Arny's wife, Kurt's aunt, Henry and Bertha's daughter-in-law

Henry, Kurt's grandfather, Bertha's husband, Johnny and Arny's father

Johnny, Kurt's father, Henry and Bertha's younger son, Arny's brother, Lorelei's husband

Kurt, Johnny and Lorelei's son, Henry and Bertha's grandson

Lena, Henry's older half sister, Otto's daughter

Lorelei, Kurt's mother, Johnny's wife, Henry and Bertha's daughter-in-law

Otto, Henry's father, Kurt's great-grandfather

List of Characters: The Others

Rodney Adenauer, Kurt's classmate in Kensington High School

Edna and Karl Boecker, the owners of a farm Henry wishes to own

Cecil Crosley, the minister at the Kensington Christian Church

Sam and Earl Gibson, the undertakers in Kensington

Claude Hagenbach, Bertha Reinhart's cousin, Gus Hagenbach's nephew

Gus Hagenbach, Bertha Reinhart's father, Claude Hagenbach's uncle

Tim Juergen, Kurt's cousin on his mother's side

Eric Larson, the owner and operator of a feed-grinding truck

Linden family, neighbors whose farm Henry buys at a mortgage foreclosure sale

Emil Olson, a trucker who hauls livestock to Chicago

Albert Rauenthaler, the owner of a farm Henry wishes to own

Riegel family, neighbors whose farm Henry buys at a mortgage foreclosure sale

Chester and Gwendolyn Smith, the owners of the Kensington State Bank

Chris Stefanovski, a student at Northern Illinois University

Warner family, neighbors whose farm Henry buys at a mortgage foreclosure sale

Part One

Kurt, Four to Ten

1947-1954

Chapter One

Kurt Reinhart often heard people accuse his grandfather, Henry Reinhart, of murder. The first time he could remember hearing the accusation was the day he turned four, which was May 16, 1947.

Thirty-five years previously, on March 3, 1912, Henry's half brother, Conrad Reinhart, had drowned in the flooding creek that ran through their farm in Kensington township in northern Illinois.

Although the Lafayette County state's attorney, citing a lack of evidence, refused to prosecute twenty-three-year-old Henry, almost everybody who heard the story was certain he'd murdered his brother.

Henry couldn't deny he'd had an opportunity to commit the crime. He and Conrad were the only persons present when the drowning occurred. Henry also had a motive. Conrad's death gave Henry undisputed title to their deceased father's farm.

The accuser at the supper table the evening Kurt's family celebrated his fourth birthday was Henry's son and Kurt's father, Johnny Reinhart.

*****

Johnny had married Kurt's mother, Lorelei Juergen, soon after they both turned eighteen. They exchanged their vows before a justice of the peace in his home on Christmas Eve in 1942.

Kurt, born less than five months later, was the reason for what the neighbors and other people who knew them said was a shotgun wedding. But the marriage didn't appear to concern Henry beyond the thirty minutes he'd spent the day before the wedding at his kitchen table with four other Reinharts and three Juergens.

The round oak table was as bare as the sky that cold afternoon. No glasses, cups or saucers—and certainly no ashtrays in Henry's house—rested upon it. The only thing the eight persons seated around it could see between them was the grain of the wood.

Henry's father, Otto Reinhart, had built the table himself, from a fallen tree.

Johnny and his mother, Bertha, were on one side of Henry. Johnny's older brother, Arny, and his sister-in-law, Elaine, were on the other. Lorelei and her parents sat across from them.

Slender Johnny and stocky Arny, having inherited their light-brown hair and eyes from both their wiry father and plump mother, were John and Arnold on their birth certificates, but only their schoolteachers used those names.

As soon as the three blond and blue-eyed guests were settled in their chairs, Henry asked them to state their case as briefly and to the point as possible.

"I've got a lot more work to do," he said, "before this day is over."

"He knew we didn't need any introductions," Bertha later told Kurt. "They'd seen us around, and we'd seen them. They were too thin, I always thought, as if they didn't have enough to eat."

The complaining family, who lived on an eighty-acre hog farm they rented in a neighboring township, included Lorelei's fifteen-year-old brother, another scrawny Juergen.

"I'm here to kill you, Johnny Reinhart!" he'd yelled, jumping out of his parents' car as soon as it had stopped in the Reinharts' driveway that afternoon.

Henry had stood at the back porch screen door and denied him entrance to the house.

Arny and Elaine quickly locked all the other doors.

From time to time nevertheless, the Reinharts and Juergens seated at the kitchen table could hear Lorelei's brother outside the house.

"He knocked her up!" he yelled. "He fucked her!"

He even made an offer to settle the matter without further ado.

"Just give me the gun!" he screamed. "I'll shoot the asshole!"

"My hunting rifle," Lorelei's father assured the Reinharts, "is locked in the trunk of our car. My son doesn't have a key to it."

The three Juergens permitted to enter the house made their argument, with more than one reminder that Johnny might have to answer to the authorities in Edinburgh, the Lafayette County seat, for what he'd done—if, of course, he refused to marry Lorelei.

After their marriage, Lorelei would live with the five Reinharts seated at the table. Lorelei's parents said they had no room in their house for Johnny and a child, even if her brother could somehow be convinced not to make good on his threat to kill Johnny.

During the remainder of Lorelei's pregnancy and thereafter, Johnny's family would provide for her. In particular, they would pay for her and her baby's medical expenses.

Their hosts heard them without making an interruption.

As soon as the Juergens finished their plea, Henry turned to Johnny and asked if he agreed to the terms their guests had laid down for him and his family.

Johnny snickered. He was neither the person with an unwanted child in her body nor the ones from whose bank account the checks would be drawn to pay for it.

He answered his father with a lustful glance at Lorelei and a quick nod of his head.

Henry turned to the Juergens. "Then that's what we'll do."

He rose from his chair. As did the other Reinharts.

"You've gotten everything you came for," Henry said, looking down on the Juergens. "I'm done with this matter."

The Juergens remained in their chairs. Was the wrong Henry Reinhart's son had inflicted upon their family not worthy of a heated confrontation?

"That means," Henry prompted his visitors, "you can leave now."

The Juergens left. The Reinharts followed them as far as the back porch to make certain Lorelei's brother, he also blue-eyed and blond, went with them.

All the way to their car, though, the Juergens kept glancing back at the Reinharts.

"I was expecting any moment," Bertha said to the others in her family shivering on their back porch as the Juergens drove off, "they'd turn to salt."

*****

Neither Henry nor Elaine attended Johnny and Lorelei's wedding ceremony.

Only Bertha and Arny appeared for the groom, only Lorelei's parents for the bride.

The wife of the justice of the peace made no attempt to conceal her amusement.

She even offered to accompany herself on her piano and sing "There Will Never Be Another You." She had the sheet music and promised she wouldn't miss a note.

"You'll think," she said, "it's a Saturday night and you're listening to *Your Hit Parade* on the radio."

That was after none of the three Reinharts present had found it necessary to respond when she'd questioned why Henry and Elaine weren't with them. Bertha, Arny and Johnny acted as if the absence of the father and sister-in-law of the groom was none of her business.

The justice of the peace quietly informed his wife he didn't think her singing would be needed for this particular wedding.

Elaine later enjoyed telling Kurt that story.

Kurt liked hearing her tell it, too. He came to call it "the story of the song never sung."

*****

After Lorelei finished her supper the first day she lived with the Reinharts, which was also her wedding day, she pulled out a cigarette and prepared to light it.

Her father-in-law reached across the table, snatched the cigarette from her lips and crushed it in his hand. Henry then took her pack of Lucky Strikes from the table in front of her and said he'd be sure to burn them the next time he made a bonfire for the garbage.

"You won't need to waste your money on these," he told his son's bride. "Not while you're living in this house."

Lorelei complied with Henry's order and gave up smoking.

"She knew she had no choice," Elaine told Kurt.

Having agreed to live with the Reinharts, Lorelei depended upon them for everything. If that meant she had to have sex with Johnny at least once every day, she'd do it. If it also meant she couldn't smoke cigarettes, she'd give them up. It got her out of what she called the "hopeless poverty" she'd suffered in her parents' house. Her brother would have to find his own way out.

*****

When Kurt was born on May 16, 1943, his grandfather owned two houses. Henry had lived all of his fifty-five years in one or the other of them.

14

His Grandfather's House

The house he'd been born in, the one up on the hill, was the house his father supposedly left him, along with his 120-acre farm, in the will Conrad contested in court up to the day he died. That house had been empty since the early 1920s.

The other house, the one down by the road, was the house Kurt's grandmother, Bertha, had grown up in. It was the house the Reinharts were living in when Kurt was born.

*****

Kurt could remember—as far back as he could remember anything, even before he was four years old—Elaine and Arny telling him what he most needed to know about his grandfather. The only thing in the world that mattered to Henry Reinhart was his farm.

In 1943, his farm was four times larger than the 120 acres he'd inherited from his father in 1911. Henry had accumulated 360 additional acres on the same section of land in Kensington township, its soil as black as coal to an exceptional depth.

But Henry believed his farm should be the whole 640-acre section. With public roads on all four of its mile-long sides, it would be his island. He'd never again have to share a fence with another human being.

The owners of the other two farms in the section, eighty acres each, were the only remaining obstacles to Henry's reaching his goal. But they'd publicly sworn they'd lay down their lives before they'd let "that Cain" add their farms to his.

Chapter Two

Johnny didn't stay around for his son's birth. Within two months of his marriage to Lorelei, he decided to enlist in the United States Army.

Henry and Bertha wanted to stop him but soon discovered they had no say in the matter. Johnny was eighteen. He still needed parental consent to marry the woman he'd impregnated but not to fight in a world war and risk losing his life.

Elaine thought Johnny had tired of his affair with Lorelei. He'd admitted to Arny their child, Kurt, six months along then, had gotten in the way of his favorite activity with her.

Johnny argued he'd soon be drafted in any event. He might as well get it over with. Besides, the recruiters told him his enlistment could keep Arny out of the draft.

Henry and Bertha remained opposed. Nevertheless, one cold, gray February morning they got in Henry's brown 1936 Pontiac to take Johnny to the train station in Edinburgh.

As they left, Elaine, on the back porch with Lorelei and Arny waving good-by, sang a popular version of the first two lines of George M. Cohan's "Over There."

"Johnny, get your gun, get your gun, get your gun. Johnny, kill the Hun, kill the Hun, kill the Hun."

Lorelei laughed.

Arny, though, said he didn't care much for that song.

*****

Johnny was soon fighting Germans as well as Italians in North Africa.

One day in the desert heat in Tunisia he looked up from the dust and saw the man running next to him, his best friend from boot camp, drop his gun, wrap his arms around his gut, stagger and fall.

Three days before Kurt was born, Johnny was present in Tunis for the Axis surrender in Africa.

More scenes of violent death followed by victory celebrations filled Johnny's days—in Sicily behind Patton's tanks, and up the boot of Italy, where every mountain he encountered exacted its own unique tribute in horror and blood.

*****

Kurt's maternal grandparents saw him once, shortly after he was born. Their visit was another story Elaine enjoyed telling Kurt.

As soon as Lorelei's mother and father stepped inside the house, they got into a loud argument with Lorelei. They said what she'd done with Johnny had ruined their lives.

Lorelei screamed back at them it was the other way around. They'd ruined *her* life. They'd forced her to have a baby she didn't want. Then they'd made her live with "these Reinharts nobody else wants anything to do with."

Lorelei's mother and father had refused to help her find somebody who could, as she'd described it to Elaine, "flush my problem down the toilet."

Whenever Elaine came to this point in her story, she'd smirk.

"My parents claimed they couldn't afford an abortion," Lorelei had told Elaine. "But I knew that was a lie. They could've borrowed the money from a bank. They'd gotten loans for less important things, like feed for my father's goddamned pigs."

For a brief while, Henry stood at the door and listened to Lorelei and her parents yell at one another. After he'd heard enough of it, though, he informed Lorelei's parents it was time for them to leave.

At first, Lorelei's mother refused to go. She complained she hadn't even held her grandson in her arms.

Henry told her she wasn't going to, either. He said she and Lorelei's father would remove themselves from his house, or he'd get his shotgun. They'd be on his property contrary to his wishes, he explained, and he'd have every right to shoot them.

Lorelei's parents chose not to wait around to find out if he'd actually do it.

"The neighbors loved that story," Elaine told Kurt, snickering herself.

With her dark brown, piercing eyes, Elaine often reminded young Kurt of an eagle. Her hair was dark brown, too, and it fell to her shoulders.

*****

His Grandfather's House

One Saturday afternoon in December of 1943, Lorelei's parents and brother were on their way to Edinburgh to shop and see a movie at the Palace.

Lorelei's brother, who'd recently obtained his driver's license on his fourth try, was behind the wheel. As he approached the railroad tracks in the village of Kensington, he sped up in an attempt to beat a freight train coming out from Chicago. Seeing he wasn't going to make it, he slammed on the brakes. The blacktop road, though, was iced over.

After the Juergens' car slid through the crossing gates, the train hit it head-on. The authorities pronounced the three Juergens dead at the scene of the accident.

*****

Bertha and Arny accompanied Lorelei to her family's triple funeral in the Kensington Christian Church with the Reverend Cecil Crosley presiding.

Elaine chose to stay home with Kurt.

Henry claimed he had too much work to do to fool his time away listening to Cecil's nonsense.

Arny and Bertha said Lorelei, who sat in the front row between them, never shed a tear. She even laughed out loud when Reverend Crosley assured the mourners her brother, who was on his high school basketball team but mostly warmed the bench, was playing the game that very moment with Jesus in heaven.

In the breath-holding silence that followed, the portly minister stared down at Lorelei through his thick, rimless glasses.

"The Lord hears your laughter," he said, pointing his finger at her. "You sinned, you grievously sinned, when you let Henry Reinhart's son have his way with you."

The Juergens' landlord claimed in probate court his former tenants owed him a large sum of money. The judge signed an order giving him the Juergens' personal property as well as the small balance they had in their checking account at the Kensington State Bank. Lorelei therefore got nothing from her parents' estate.

Their life insurance only paid for their and her brother's burial expenses, even after Lorelei refused to let a cent of it go to Cecil for what she said was "his insulting funeral service."

19

Bertha felt obliged to send Cecil her check for his bill.

*****

Soon after the triple funeral, Lorelei began spending time with a man.

He'd pull his Cadillac into the Reinharts' driveway, and she'd be waiting for him in the screened-in back porch no matter how cold the weather was.

Elaine would peek at them from behind the curtains of a window facing the driveway.

She could see Lorelei's friend wore expensive suits and gold cufflinks.

This was yet another story Elaine was as pleased to tell as Kurt was to hear.

"He didn't shop for his clothes and accessories at Sears," she said.

"How old was he?" Kurt asked.

"Around thirty," Elaine guessed, "give or take a year or two."

Arny and Bertha, who sometimes joined Elaine behind the curtains, confirmed that assessment.

"Actually," Elaine told Kurt more than once, "your mother's boyfriend was almost as good-looking as your father was."

"Yes, he was," Arny agreed. "He'd get out of his car and open the door for Lorelei. A real Prince Charming, he was. He didn't look to me as if he'd ever done farmwork. But he'd kept himself in good shape even so. He must've exercised a lot."

"We can well imagine," Elaine said, laughing, "what some of his exercise consisted of."

Lorelei told the Reinharts the man was a lawyer who lived and worked in Edinburgh. He was also, she claimed, a cousin. He'd promised her at the triple funeral, she said, he'd do whatever he could to help her through her grief.

Neither Arny nor Bertha had seen him at the funeral. And they were both certain they would've noticed anybody "that striking."

They agreed with Elaine. The man was no relative of Lorelei's.

He was, though, the attorney she'd gone to see the day after the funeral.

His Grandfather's House

Lorelei confided to Elaine he was holding back his tears when he advised her she had no defense to the landlord's claim against her parents' estate and no viable suit against the railroad for the deaths of her parents and brother. The railroad had found people who'd seen her brother speed up to beat the train. The witnesses had also sworn in affidavits the signals and gates were working properly.

"That lawyer should've tried acting in the movies," Elaine loved to say during this part of the story. "He wasn't holding back his tears. He wasn't looking for a woman with money of her own. He wanted Lorelei for the same reason Johnny had wanted her. She was young, pretty and poor—and she put out."

Chapter Three

The neighbors knew why Lorelei could cavort with a boyfriend in her husband's absence and get away with it.

"Those Reinharts," they agreed, "just don't give a damn about that sort of thing."

Bertha and Arny made no mention of Lorelei's friend in their letters to Johnny.

Elaine and Henry didn't write letters to Johnny, or he to them.

*****

Johnny fought for more than two years in Africa and Europe without coming home. A drunken fight in a liberated village on his way to Rome brought an end to his days in Italy. The army sent him to England to take part in D-Day.

The neighbors argued whether the move was meant to punish Johnny or to increase the chances for a successful invasion.

During the battle, Johnny jumped off a landing boat and ran across a beach under fire.

"I was damned lucky," Johnny later told his son at the supper table before his fourth-birthday party began. "Our guys up in the air saved my life."

Johnny moved his hands, his index fingers spinning like propellers, just above Kurt's mop of light-brown hair.

"They bombed the embankments," Johnny explained. "That's where those damned krauts were with their machine guns waiting to mow down my buddies and me."

Johnny aimed an imaginary machine gun at a spot on his son's forehead midway between his light-brown eyes and shot him dead numerous times, to Kurt's great amusement.

After the bombed German soldiers died their horrifying deaths—their body parts lying like crimson flowers in a garden wherever Johnny looked—he and his buddies ran into France, all of them still alive.

*****

Johnny had only one opportunity for a drunken weekend in Paris. Hitler's Christmas surprise in the Ardennes forest brought Johnny to Belgium and the Battle of the Bulge. But after the bleakest winter of his life by far, he found himself in the Netherlands in the spring. He became aware he might survive the war and wake up home again like Garland in that movie.

But he first needed to fight in Germany.

"The natives call it something like Doichlant," he told his son.

It was the Deutschland all four of his grandparents had left in their youth.

By the time the war in Europe came to an end in May of 1945, Johnny had won an impressive array of battle ribbons. Yet the highest rank he ever attained was private first class.

The story told in Kensington explained the conundrum. Too many drunken nights and too many barroom brawls had resulted in too many busts in rank and pay.

"People ask me," Arny said at the supper table one evening, "was it a miracle none of those German or Italian bullets ever hit Johnny? Or was it just dumb luck?"

Henry scoffed. "Only fools believe in miracles. And luck is always dumb. Otherwise, it wouldn't be luck."

"Well, I don't care what it was," Bertha said, glaring at Henry. "Johnny's coming home. He's my son, and I wish to see him again alive. Whether it was a miracle or luck, I'll take it."

*****

Shortly before Johnny returned from Europe in the autumn of 1945, the man Lorelei had gone out with closed his office in Edinburgh and moved to Los Angeles.

The Reinharts still refused to say anything about him to Johnny.

Their neighbors, though, weren't reluctant to mention to him that Lorelei and her lawyer, if that's what he was, usually conducted their business dealings, if that's what they were, after normal working hours. And why, they asked, did she need an attorney anyway, after he'd delivered the sad news regarding her parents' probate proceeding and her wrongful death claim against the railroad?

When Johnny confronted Lorelei, she told him the same story she'd told the other Reinharts. The man was a cousin who'd kindly befriended her and seen her through her grief.

His Grandfather's House

She denied her lawyer cousin had closed his office and moved away because he knew Johnny was coming home. She said he'd always wanted to live in Southern California. He hated Midwestern winters. He'd recently won a large settlement for a client in a personal injury suit and saw his chance to get out of Edinburgh.

"And I say," Lorelei chose to add, "good for him."

*****

Early one morning in the spring of 1947, Lorelei drove off in Henry's 1936 Pontiac. She was on her way to Kensington with Elaine's list of the groceries the Reinharts needed.

Lorelei didn't return.

Later that day somebody found the car parked on the side of a rarely traveled road. The key was under the front seat where the Reinharts always kept it.

After hearing the news, Elaine went up to Johnny and Lorelei's room on the second floor of the house. A quick inspection of the closet and chest of drawers revealed that her sister-in-law's suitcases, clothes and all her other personal belongings were gone.

Lorelei must've placed them in the trunk of the car the previous night, while the six other occupants of the house slept.

Her activities had somehow failed to rouse even Johnny, who shared her bed.

"The alcohol in him would explain that," Elaine said.

The next time Elaine and Arny drove to Kensington, for the groceries Lorelei hadn't brought home, they scarcely had time to park the car on Main Street before they learned something else.

And the neighbors and townspeople who delivered the news were either unable or unwilling to keep themselves from revealing how much they enjoyed it.

Some of them told the story openly laughing.

Lorelei's friend, still driving a late-model Cadillac, had returned to Edinburgh that week. His brief visit ended, though, the day Lorelei disappeared.

The Reinharts had been aware of the letters Lorelei had received from him in California and of those she'd placed in the roadside mailbox for him.

*****

The following Sunday, Bertha, who'd wept upon learning her younger daughter-in-law had run away, chose to attend the morning service at the Kensington Christian Church.

Arny went with her. He paid no more attention to what Cecil had to say than his father did, but he'd never let his mother go to church alone.

The Reverend Crosley seldom took his eyes off them during his sermon.

They hadn't noticed the lengthy sermon title on the sign in front of the church that day—"The Proper Response of Christians to Sin Committed in Their Presence."

"Do they go about their lives as if nothing has happened?" Cecil thundered. "No! Do they refuse to inform a husband his wife is engaged in illicit relations with another man? No! Could they even imagine holding their tongues if the husband was their son or brother bravely fighting for their country across the sea? No! A thousand times no!"

An unusual number of people—who'd correctly guessed what was to come but never imagined Bertha and Arny would be present for it—attended church that morning. Some of them had to sit in folding chairs along the back wall, in the aisles and down in front below the pulpit.

When Bertha and Arny passed the collection plate without putting anything in it, Cecil took note, raising his voice enough to be heard above the organist's vigorous rendition of "Onward, Christian Soldiers."

"Obstinate refusal to admit error," he said, "is itself a sin. God can see what we do—and what we don't do!"

"You can treat yourselves to something nice," Elaine reassured Arny and Bertha, "with the money you didn't put in the collection plate."

Henry had nothing to say. What he called Cecil's attention-seeking ravings were beneath his notice, even when the reverend aimed them at him and his family.

Chapter Four

Johnny's ribbons from the war brought on the argument he got into with Elaine at the supper table the day Kurt turned four.

Less than three weeks had passed since Lorelei had run off with her lawyer friend and left her son with his Reinhart relatives.

Johnny, holding Kurt on his lap, had spread the ribbons on the table in front of them.

Elaine, who was setting the table, asked Johnny to put his ribbons away.

"Just wait a goddamned minute," Johnny said.

Johnny was twenty-two. He'd fought in the greatest war of them all and come home from it without suffering a physical wound more severe than the few cuts and bruises inflicted by an ill-chosen opponent in the bar fight in Italy.

Arny had watched his brother go up to the old house on the hill early that afternoon. Johnny kept his whiskey there.

"I want my boy to see my ribbons," Johnny insisted.

"We're ready to eat," Elaine said. "The war's over and done with. It's time to put your ribbons away. They never did you any good. They certainly didn't impress Lorelei enough to keep her from running off with Prince Charming. You know, that young, single, childless, able-bodied lawyer who for some reason didn't have to fight in the war."

Since Henry hadn't come into the house yet, Elaine and Johnny were free to snap at one another all they wished. Bertha and Arny knew they couldn't stop them even if they tried.

"Lorelei might've run away," Johnny said, "but she didn't run away from me."

"Oh, she didn't?" Elaine asked. "And here I thought you were her husband."

"She ran away from you people," Johnny insisted.

"From us?" Bertha asked. "Why would she run away from us?"

"She always complained," her younger son said with the tears of a drunk in his eyes, "you people watched over her like hawks during the war. She told me she hated living here. She would've been happier in a prison. That's why she ran off. I should've taken her away as soon as I came home. I know that's what she wanted me to do."

"It's a good thing you're drunk," Elaine said, "and we don't have to take you seriously. We didn't watch over Lorelei like hawks. We were more like doves. We let her do whatever she damned well pleased.

Not one of us ever said a word to her about her boyfriend."

Elaine was working over the new electric stove Henry had bought, claiming until the moment he made the purchase it would be an unforgiveable waste of money.

The first few days after Lorelei left, Johnny had gone up to the house on the hill before breakfast.

"You didn't care how she felt here, living with you," he persisted. "I don't know what good it did for me to go off and fight in that goddamned war. I should've stayed home. I sure as hell made a big mistake leaving my wife here so you people could turn her against me. She was too young and pretty, and you all hated her for that. You were jealous of her."

"Me?" Bertha asked. "Are you saying I was jealous of Lorelei? I certainly never thought I was. She was always nice to me. I liked her. I believe she liked me."

Elaine looked at Johnny and laughed. "You turned Lorelei against you all by yourself. You acted as if you owned her, for one purpose only. When that didn't work out, you ran off to war and whore, as they say. And came home a hopeless drunk."

Johnny had clung to the view that the man Lorelei had gone out with was just what she'd said he was: a harmless, good-hearted cousin. And Johnny was certain Lorelei would soon come back from wherever she'd gone. So what if she wanted to visit a relative in California? Johnny only wished, he'd told Arny one day, she'd asked him to go with her.

"You like to talk," Johnny said, looking at Elaine. "That's all you and the people around here know how to do. You didn't go off and fight in the war. You sat home nice and cozy and dreamed up stories to tell one another, so you could pass the days and make them halfway interesting. So you wouldn't get more bored with yourselves than you already were."

"I think," Elaine said, scooping up Johnny's war ribbons and handing them to Bertha, "you'd better face the truth. That man your Lorelei went out with while you were away wasn't some helpful relative. He was her boyfriend. And I'm sure she was doing with him exactly what she was doing with you when you were her boyfriend. She didn't give a damn if she had a husband off fighting in a war or an infant child her in-laws were taking care of."

His Grandfather's House

Smelling of that day's sweat and bourbon, Johnny sat slumped in his chair, clinging to his four-year-old son like a Christian hugging Jesus on the road to heaven.

*****

Kurt's grandfather let the screen door to the back porch slam shut behind him.

Nobody in the kitchen had anything more to say about Johnny's absent wife.

Henry took his seat at the table.

Kurt sat where he always did, in the chair to the right of his grandfather's. Henry was right-handed and cut his grandson's beefsteak and pork chops into tiny morsels for him.

Kurt had a cushion on his chair that raised him up to the table. Bertha and Arny had found it for him at the Sears store in Edinburgh.

At fifty-nine, Henry had a full head of graying hair, a face without any sagging skin or wrinkles, and a body lean and still remarkably graceful.

After Elaine's platters of roast beef, red potatoes, carrots and onions and Bertha's bowl of gravy had made one full circuit around the table, Henry noticed Johnny's plate was bare except for a single slice of beef with some gravy on it.

"It's no wonder your wife left you," Henry said to his younger son. "I can't say I blame her. Every day since you got home, you've been drunk. And I know why you drink. It was that goddamned war. You were too young to go off and fight in it. And for what? So you could come home to your family with your brain so addled you don't know what you're doing? Well, God bless America. You certainly did your duty to it. No one can complain about that."

Bertha held a dish towel to her face and wept.

Arny closed his eyes.

Henry continued, looking at Johnny. "You'll have to figure out whether you want to be of better use around here or you want to drink. The rest of us can work this farm without you. We did when you were off fighting in that war, and we'll do it again. I appreciate your help when you're sober. But you'll have to make up your mind whether you wish to stay here and work the way you used to or go somewhere else and drink yourself silly."

Even as early as his fourth birthday, Kurt knew he was supposed to listen carefully whenever Henry spoke. His grandmother had told him his grandfather expected the members of his family to be like the people God spoke to in the Bible—obedient.

When the time came for dessert, Bertha placed in front of Kurt a German chocolate cake with a double layer of frosting. She'd made it that day. She laid four candles and a box of wooden matches in front of Johnny, who was sitting on the other side of his son.

Johnny stared at the cake as if he didn't know what it was.

Henry looked at Bertha. "Will you please put the candles on your cake and light them?"

"I thought," Bertha said, "Kurt's father should do it."

"What sort of nonsense is that?" Henry asked. "If you don't want to do it, let Elaine do it. I've got more work to do before it's dark. We've got to be in the fields as early tomorrow as we can. By this time last year, we had all our corn planted."

Johnny picked up the candles one at a time and stuck them in the cake. When he was done, the candles didn't form a nice level square in the middle of the cake, but a highly irregular trapezoid with its tilted corners rising to various heights above the frosting.

Elaine put her hand to her mouth to hide her grin.

Arny, sitting on the other side of his brother, slid open the box of matches, but Johnny grabbed it from him.

"He's my boy!" Johnny yelled.

"Let Arny do that," Henry ordered his younger son. "You're shaking so much you'll burn the house down. You're too damned drunk to light those candles."

Johnny glared at his father. "You'd be drunk, too, if you'd had to do what I did in that fucking war. You only had to kill one person, your silly old brother, a goddamned drunk like me, and you got yourself a farm out of it. What the fuck did I get for sailing across the ocean and killing all those goddamned krauts and dagos?"

Johnny threw the box of matches down on the table, lifted Kurt up from his chair and carried him out the door to the back porch.

"Bring that boy back here!" Henry yelled.

Kurt, who was afraid he'd fall, clung to Johnny.

Johnny, sobbing, sat down on the single cement step outside the screen door.

Elaine called it "the hobo step" because it was where Bertha asked tramps from the road to sit when they ate whatever they were able to beg from her, which was often an ample meal.

When Johnny failed to return Kurt to the table, Henry got up from his chair, charged across the kitchen and the porch, threw open the screen door, grabbed his grandson by his outstretched hands, and carried him back inside the house.

Arny, having rearranged the candles on the birthday cake, lit them.

Johnny didn't return to watch Kurt blow them out the way his grandmother said he was supposed to, all with one breath.

*****

The house up on the hill had gone unpainted for the quarter of a century it stood empty. It lacked indoor plumbing and electrical wiring. In the summer, its two stories appeared low against the sky to people climbing the dirt path that led to it. But they soon saw the effect was due to the overgrown bushes and other vegetation surrounding it.

The morning after Kurt's birthday supper, Arny, on his way to the barn to do the usual chores, noticed the back door to the old house was hanging open.

At the fork in the path, where the lilac his grandfather Otto had planted was in full bloom, he stopped, glanced at his father trudging down to the barn, and looked up at the house one more time.

Elaine had nudged him awake during the night and claimed she'd heard an explosion. Arny had heard nothing and soon fell asleep again.

But now he ran up the path. He remembered the shotgun his father had fired at horse thieves one night during the First World War. The blasts sent them running away from the barn and across the creek.

As frightened as he was initially, five-year-old Arny had ended up laughing. The would-be thieves splashed through the water, stumbled on the stones they couldn't see in the dark, and cursed one another for getting in the way.

Bertha had begged Henry long ago not to keep his gun in the house they lived in down by the road. Acceding to her wishes, he'd left it in the house on the hill.

He'd also kept it in good repair, despite its age, and loaded.

Arny found his brother's body in a dusty room upstairs.

He didn't have to be a police detective to see Johnny had placed the ends of both barrels of the gun in his mouth. Then he'd pulled—no, pushed—the triggers and blown off his head.

Chapter Five

Henry's father, Otto, had chosen the flat top of the hill at the southern edge of his farm for the location of his house as well as his orchard, vineyard, berry patches and garden. His family sold fruits and vegetables at a stand down by the road from May to October.

Otto had four children to help him. When Henry took over the farm upon his father's death, though, he was on his own. His half brother, Conrad, murdered or not, was soon dead himself.

Henry's half sisters, Cora and Lena, who were Conrad's full sisters and in their seventies then, claimed they were too old to do the farm and garden work they'd done for their father. They said Henry, who'd inherited the farm, could keep them alive or not as he saw fit, but in no event would they do the work they used to do.

Henry decided to give up on his father's produce business. His cattle and hogs were far more profitable than the fruits, vegetables, cider and wine Otto had sold at his roadside stand.

After Henry married Bertha, she reclaimed a part of Otto's garden from the weeds growing in its place. She also picked the strawberries, cherries, blackberries, raspberries, blueberries, plums, apples, pears and grapes continuing to ripen in what gradually became more of a thicket than a cultivated hilltop. Henry told her he was sorry, but he couldn't assist her. He had farmland to work and livestock to feed.

When Johnny grew old enough to do farmwork, Arny began helping his mother tend her garden and harvest whatever they could find in the thicket.

The hill on which Otto had situated his house was the only elevated area in Lafayette County. Otto told Henry he'd decided from his reading it was a moraine, a mound of debris left behind when the glaciers retreated at the end of the Ice Age.

Whatever it was, Otto's hilltop included a family burial ground. When Johnny killed himself in 1947, more than a quarter of a century had passed since the Reinharts had last opened a grave in it.

*****

Henry and Arny dug the grave for Johnny the same day Arny found him in the old house. That Saturday afternoon was unusually warm for May.

Bertha and Elaine walked up the hill to the burial ground. Each carried a Mason jar filled with ice water and wrapped in a kitchen towel. Kurt dawdled along behind them.

This was another of his earliest memories. His grandfather and uncle were for some reason digging a hole at the far end of the orchard. His grandmother had told him he was going to a funeral, whatever that might be. The pretty young woman his relatives had said was his mother had disappeared. Up in the old house that frightened Kurt every time he went near it, something terrible had happened to Johnny, the playful man whose odor Elaine and Bertha sometimes objected to but Kurt didn't mind.

"Reverend Crosley called," Bertha said after she, Elaine and Kurt had reached the burial ground. "He wants to hold a funeral service for Johnny on Monday morning. He'll do it for free."

She handed her jar down to Henry in their younger son's grave.

He took a long drink from it before he spoke.

"You want that man to hold a funeral for your son?" he asked, not bothering to conceal his disgust.

"I do," Bertha replied. "We can't put Johnny in the ground without a service."

"If he's in a casket, we can," Henry said. "The Gibsons told me that's all the law requires us to do."

Sam and Earl Gibson were the undertakers in Kensington. They'd inherited the business from their father.

Henry wasn't done. "And after what Cecil said the last time you went to church?"

Bertha fought back tears. "I don't care what Crosley says about us. I just want a funeral service for Johnny."

Arny handed his water jar to Elaine, hoisted himself up out of Johnny's grave and threw his arms around his mother.

Henry glanced at the cloudless sky above them.

"I only hope," he said, "the next rain holds off until Monday. As soon as we get this hole dug, we'll go back to planting corn. We'll plant tomorrow, too."

He took another long drink of his water.

"Now that Johnny's gone," he said, "we'll need every minute we can get. I won't rest until we've finished the planting."

After handing his Mason jar to Elaine, he dug down with his

spade as if he bore a grudge against the earth itself.

"Last night," Elaine couldn't help reminding her father-in-law, "you told Johnny we could get by just fine without him. Isn't that why he killed himself?"

"Elaine," Arny whispered.

Henry dug into the clay again as if he hadn't heard Elaine.

Bertha looked down at Henry's cattle and hogs roaming the floor of the valley along the creek and the wooded slopes on either side of it. That was so she could take her eyes off Johnny's grave and the mound of earth piled beside it.

Bertha seldom removed her glasses. When Kurt saw her with them off, she looked as if her face were incomplete.

"Johnny," she said, her voice unsteady, "helped as much as he could. It wasn't his fault that war drove him to drink."

Elaine wasn't about to waste any of her tears on Johnny.

"I remember him drinking too much," she said, "before he left to fight the war."

"Elaine," Arny responded softly, attempting to soothe. "You shouldn't talk like that."

He glanced at his mother.

"Not now," he said.

Henry kept digging.

"The people who lead us in high office," he said, "are good at one thing only—whipping the rest of the people into frenzies. They scooped up Johnny in their last goddamned madness. This country should've stood by and watched while those lunatics in Europe and Asia bled one another dry. It would've ended up best for us. We had no business sending our young men and treasure all over the world to fight other peoples' battles."

This wasn't the first time Henry's family had had the benefit of his isolationist opinions. America's ally in the last war, Stalin's Soviet Union, which had now become its most dangerous enemy, only proved, Henry liked to say, the wisdom of his views. His father's adopted land could've avoided Pearl Harbor, he argued, by letting Japan create its empire in East Asia—and suffer the inevitable wrath of its subjugated neighbors in the years to come.

He emptied his spade on the mound of earth beside the grave—some of it perhaps debris from the Ice Age—and looked up at Elaine.

"The pitiful, drunken Johnny who came home from that war," Henry said, "wasn't the boy who went over there. He wasn't Lorelei's husband or this boy's father. All that killing he saw changed him into something different."

Kurt blinked. Did he or did he not, he wondered, have a father? If he had one, where was he? And where was Lorelei's husband? Where was Lorelei? Where was Johnny?

Elaine and Arny stared at Henry.

"That goddamned war," Kurt's grandfather continued, "killed Johnny just as much as it did those boys who died in the fighting. He just took longer to die from it. That's the only difference between them and him."

A warm breeze from the south rippled through the burial ground grass, which already came up to Kurt's waist.

"We should replace Lena's headstone," his grandmother said.

Lena's was the second stone east of the new grave. It was broken just above the ground, and the top of it lay in the grass like a fairy-tale door to another world.

There were four more stones beyond Lena's. Johnny's would be the seventh in his grandfather's orchard cemetery.

Henry glanced at his half sister's stone.

"We'll do it in the fall," he said, "after we get the crops in, before it snows. We'll replace hers and set a new one for Johnny at the same time."

Taking care of his half sister's headstone, maintaining his father's orchard, digging his son's grave—for Henry Reinhart those tasks were distractions. They didn't move him a hairsbreadth closer to the consummation of his vision. Only arduous, day-after-day work tending his fields and livestock could accomplish that.

Chapter Six

Monday morning in the Kensington Christian Church, Elaine, Arny, Bertha and Kurt occupied the short center pew in the first row.

The honor guard from the American Legion, in the uniforms they'd worn home in 1945, occupied the front pews on either side of the family.

"You could see at a glance," Elaine remarked later, with a laugh, "how much weight they'd put on since the war. I'm sure Johnny's uniform would've still fit him perfectly."

The stained-glass windows of the church were wide open. A lot of field work could've been accomplished that warm, sunny morning. Nevertheless, every pew in the church and every folding chair was filled. A line of mourners stood at the back of the church as well.

They'd read about Johnny's suicide in a front-page article in the Sunday morning edition of the *Edinburgh Times,* below a photograph of the deceased in his uniform and a headline, "WAR HERO KILLS SELF." The Lafayette County sheriff had confirmed that Johnny's death was "by his own hand," following the "mysterious disappearance of his young wife."

After the choir sang "The Rock of Ages" and "Nearer, my God, to Thee," the assembled onlookers, sitting and standing, got what they came for. And it wasn't Reverend Crosley's usual funeral sermon.

"We face a most vexing question," he began, extending his open hands outward toward the congregation. "I put it to you as children of God."

Cecil, in his late sixties then, was a tall man with thinning gray hair.

"I put this question to myself," he said, now holding his arms in front of himself as if they were the folded wings of an angel, "your humble and somewhat troubled pastor."

Suddenly, though, Cecil's hands, eyes and voice went heavenward.

"I put this question to God Almighty our Lord."

On cue, the organist struck a single mournful key.

"Suppose a young man dies," Cecil resumed, looking down at the Reinharts. "Suppose the young man has lived among us no more than twenty-two years. Suppose the lad is raised in a Christian community but in total ignorance of the Christian faith. Suppose even, unthinkable as it might seem, that doesn't matter to his family. I ask you, can such an unfortunate young man as I describe hope to enter the eternal kingdom of heaven? Can Private First Class Johnny Reinhart?"

The persons attending Johnny's funeral knew Henry Reinhart wasn't religious. Some said—Reverend Crosley was one of them—it took a person with no faith in Christ to do what Henry had done.

When Arny was a child, Bertha took him to Sunday school at the Kensington Christian Church. When he reached his teens, though—in the 1920s, after Johnny was born—he asked his father if he had to continue his attendance.

"No," Henry replied. "You choose to go or not go, as you see fit."

Bertha didn't disagree.

Johnny never went to church, not even for the holidays.

Every Christmas when Arny and Johnny were growing up, Bertha decorated an evergreen tree she'd planted outside the middle of the three living room windows facing the road. She placed gifts for her sons on a table inside the window. She made it clear to them, though, the presents didn't come from some Santa Claus as rewards for their good behavior. They came from her because she would always love them no matter what they did.

Having posed his most vexing question, Reverend Crosley launched upon a narrative of Johnny Reinhart's military service in the war. Chasing Rommel out of Africa. Storming Salerno beaches. Breaking through at Monte Casino. Liberating Rome. Invading Normandy beaches. Liberating France. Driving on to the Elbe. And celebrating, only two years ago in another May, the ultimate victory over America's enemies in Europe.

Cecil had used Johnny's battle ribbons to put together the story he told from his pulpit.

From the beginning to the end of the war, Cecil had avidly read the *Chicago Tribune*'s reports from the various fronts. He daily followed the lines on the maps separating Allied from Axis forces. He watched them move across countries and continents.

"One can see," he'd told his congregation, "that the hand of God Himself draws those lines. One can find in these maps the ultimate proof that God sheds His grace on America!"

Now he imagined the role of Johnny Reinhart in those historic and epic battles.

"His comrade every step of his way," Cecil proclaimed, "was Jesus Christ Himself!"

"Amen!" the choir director declared.

"How else," Cecil asked, "could Johnny have escaped the slightest scratch on his body despite the thousands of bullets the enemy fired at him? I say this young man achieved a miracle in the battles he fought. He proved nothing less than the existence of the God we worship!"

Cecil, who'd been Kensington's only minister for the last thirty-five years, lifted his eyes from the closed casket and turned to the Reinharts.

"I say," he continued, filling the church with his voice, "the man within this coffin saved our beloved America from the predations of the devil, Lucifer, Satan, call him what you will."

The mourners tittered. Cecil knew what they'd come to hear.

"But it isn't for me to speculate," he said, "on what further evil befell this young patriot after he came home. We'll never know, the way God knows, what was done to bring on Johnny Reinhart's tragic death, or what could've been done to prevent it. But I do know what killed this young hero who survived the deadliest war ever fought. What killed Johnny Reinhart was the evil we confront from those who live among us as if God doesn't exist!"

The congregation murmured.

"Mind you," Cecil went on, "I speak not of the petty evil wrought by those who are merely weak in their faith."

He allowed himself the briefest of glances at the mourners beyond the Reinharts.

"I speak," he said, "of the evil implanted among us by those who refuse to believe!"

"Amen!" the choir director and more than a few of the mourners cried.

"I return to my question," Cecil said, lifting his eyes again and lowering his voice. "Dear God, can this lad who died, oh, too young, hope to enter Your eternal kingdom?"

Cecil continued looking upward in silence, finally nodding as if he'd heard the answer.

"I say Johnny can," he said. "Our God is a merciful God. Our

God is a forgiving God. And who would be more suitable for God to forgive than this brave lad in this flag-draped coffin? He was kept from a knowledge of God against his will. And yet, despite his innocence, he saw what evil was and volunteered to vanquish it."

Cecil paused to let his words sink in. The mourners knew Henry hadn't wanted either of his sons to fight in the war.

"The lesson of this tragedy," Cecil continued, "the lesson of this young man's brief life and early death is clear. We can thwart evil wherever it resides, even in its own house!"

"Amen!" many of the mourners called out.

Cecil turned his back on the Reinharts and motioned to the choir director.

The funeral sermon was over. It was time for another hymn.

The choir and the mourners sang this one, "Amazing Grace," together.

They had no doubt who the "wretch like me" in it was.

*****

The Reinharts who'd attended Johnny's funeral service followed the uniformed men from the honor guard who carried his casket out of the church and down the front steps.

Henry, wearing the clothes he wore working on his farm, stood with the Gibson brothers next to their new black hearse.

Kurt ran to him. Henry picked him up and took him in his arms.

After the men chosen to be the coffin bearers slid it into the hearse, Reverend Crosley turned to Arny.

"Might the honor guard and I," he asked, "accompany your brother to his burial plot?"

The mourners, who'd spilled out of the church onto the front steps, lawn and even the street, fell silent.

Arny shook his head. "No, I'm afraid not. My father wants to keep the burial service private."

The minister peered at Henry. "I'm aware that's your father's wish. But I thought perhaps if just Johnny's young friends in the honor guard and I attended, the service would still be private."

Henry, holding Kurt in his arms, glared at Cecil and shook his head. "You won't do any of your carny show performance over my son

40

on my farm."

As the most cynical spectators snickered, a man wearing an *Edinburgh Times* name tag took a photo. The flash momentarily blinded Kurt.

"If you dare set foot on my property," Henry said to Cecil, "either the sheriff, if he sends his deputies, or my shotgun, if he doesn't, will resolve the matter."

Many in the crowd gasped. The newspaper articles and radio newscasts on Johnny's death had all revealed he'd killed himself with his father's shotgun.

The Kensington Christian Church was nondenominational. Cecil had inherited it from his father, who'd organized it. The reverend did as his father had done. He spent the offerings as he saw fit. Mostly for his family when his two daughters were still at home and his wife was alive. Mostly, after that, for himself.

Cecil claimed no law could ever prohibit him from doing what he did. The First Amendment guaranteed, he said, precisely what his Kensington Christian Church was—the free exercise of religion.

And nobody agreed with him more than Henry Reinhart.

"That windbag," he later told Kurt, "is entitled to make as much money off those suckers as they're willing to drop on his collection plate. No law should stop him or them from doing what they do. Everybody in this world should be free to play the fool."

*****

Sam and Earl Gibson brought Johnny out to the farm. They, Henry, Arny, Elaine and Bertha removed the coffin from the hearse and carried it up to the orchard.

Kurt, obeying his grandfather, walked a distance behind the coffin. He could see how all of them except his grandfather and Elaine struggled.

The Gibson brothers and the four adult Reinharts, using ropes, lowered the coffin into the new grave next to Cora's. Henry and Arny picked up their spades and shoveled the earth back into the hole they'd dug.

The photo of Cecil, Henry and Kurt appeared on the front page of Tuesday's *Edinburgh Times* beneath the headline, "FATHER VILIFIED AT WAR HERO'S FUNERAL."

Chapter Seven

Kurt and his grandfather had their heavy winter coats on in Edna and Karl Boecker's kitchen. It was a Saturday afternoon in February of 1953. The previous month, General Dwight Eisenhower, Johnny's supreme commander in North Africa and Europe, had become president.

Edna put her hands on the table in front of her and struggled to rise from her chair.

Kurt got up from his chair, took her elbows in his hands and helped her to her feet.

Her wrinkled face close to Kurt's, Edna chuckled.

"Thank you," she said. "You made that seem easy, even with my ample bottom."

After Kurt let her go and took his chair again, she hobbled over to her cast-iron cook stove, leaned down, pulled the fuel door open and looked back at him.

Kurt imagined himself Hansel, and Edna the witch waiting to roast him in her oven.

"You must be old enough," she said, "to help with the farmwork."

"He is," Henry said. "He does his chores without being asked."

Edna picked up one of the pails of corncobs the Boeckers kept behind their stove. She emptied it in the stove with one surprisingly quick toss. The dying fire caught the dry cobs and flared back to life.

Edna slammed the door shut.

She stood for a moment by the stove and looked at Kurt again.

"How old are you?" she asked.

"I'll be ten in May," Kurt replied.

"You look older than ten," she said.

She turned and peered at her blanket-covered chair as if it were a destination in a dream.

"Reinharts make their sons do outside work," she said, "when other boys their age are still in the house with their mamas and sisters."

She started back to her chair. Each step made her wince.

"Well, that's the difference," she went on, glancing at Kurt's grandfather. "You and Bertha had two boys. Now you've got this grandson. That's the difference right there."

Elaine had told Kurt the Boeckers couldn't have children.

"Karl couldn't," Elaine said. "There wasn't anything wrong with

Edna. Karl had a bad case of the mumps when he was eighteen. It made him sterile. People say Edna didn't find out about it until after she'd married him."

Edna sat down in her chair again and pulled her blankets around her.

"If we'd had children," she said, after she'd settled herself, "they'd be here now taking care of us. But the way it is, with no children, well, there isn't anything anybody can do for Karl and Edna Boecker."

"No," Kurt's grandfather said, "that isn't right. You own valuable farmland. You own it free and clear. You and Karl can do a lot for yourselves with the money that will bring you."

Edna looked at Kurt and laughed. "Did you know your grandpa was a good-looking young man? All the girls his age pined for him. At least until that nasty business with his older half brother came along."

"If you need any help here in your house," Henry said, ignoring her remarks, "you just let us know. If I can't come myself, I'll send Kurt over. I'm damned sure he'll do whatever you want done."

"Karl and I appreciate the assistance your family has given us," Edna said, turning to Henry. "But it isn't the same as it would be if we had our own children to help us."

Edna and Henry gazed at one another across the kitchen table.

They both knew she and Karl had something Henry craved, an eighty-acre farm in a corner of the section he'd decided should be entirely his.

The Boeckers' farm was a half-mile long north and south and a quarter-mile wide west and east. Their deed described it as "the west half of the northwest quarter" of the section.

Kurt had read that Thomas Jefferson had dreamed up the division of American land beyond the original thirteen colonies. He did it with square-mile sections and six-square-mile townships containing thirty-six sections.

Jefferson, the author of the Declaration of Independence and the third American president, also owned slaves.

*****

Kurt spent evenings after supper with his grandfather at the table in their kitchen. Kurt would be deep into the books he'd brought home from school. A few of them were the easy textbooks his teachers required him and his classmates to read. Most of them, though, were books he'd checked out of the library because their first two or three pages promised him something new and interesting.

Henry would update his account books and carefully peruse the *Chicago Tribune* and any other publications he'd received that day. When he was done with all that, he'd pick up the most recent edition of the Lafayette County Farm Bureau's book of plat maps, turn to the page for Kensington township and point his finger at Section 28. He'd shake his head when he saw the two eighty-acre farms that kept him from owning the whole square mile.

Edna and Karl Boecker's west half of the northwest quarter was one. Albert Rauenthaler's "west half of the northeast quarter" was the other.

*****

"We'll be dead pretty soon," Edna Boecker said. "I can feel it in my bones. So can he."

She motioned toward the man in the corner by the stove. He was sitting under his blankets in an easy chair that at one time, maybe forty years ago, stood new in their living room.

He'd complained, as soon as Kurt and his grandfather had entered the house, something was wrong with the stove.

"The damned thing," he said, "ain't giving off near enough heat."

A few minutes later, though, the pleasantries over, he resumed snoring.

He and Edna both had full heads of straight white hair. Hers was only an inch or so longer than his.

The previous August the dairy cows the Boeckers kept had broken through a fence Karl and Edna had neglected to mend for a dozen years or more. The animals got onto the Reinharts' property. Henry, Elaine, Arny and Kurt ended up chasing the cattle through the corn that evening.

"It was so dark in there we couldn't see," Elaine told her mother-in-law. "And every time one of those big leaves hit you just right it was like a knife."

45

Karl Boecker had attempted to help, but within minutes he was panting and wheezing.

"It's just the pollen," he tried to explain, but Henry told him to stay out of the field.

Ordinarily, Henry would've sworn and raved, for all to hear, about anything as monstrous as cows in his corn, but that night chasing the Boeckers' cattle he made no complaint at all.

"Then who's going to see to it," Edna asked at her kitchen table six months later, shuddering, "we're properly buried? If we go in the winter, we'll be left dead in this house for months. God only knows how long it'll be before they find us."

She looked around her as if she were already in her tomb.

"That's nonsense, and you know it," Kurt's grandfather said. "You both have another twenty years, at least, to live. And we'll be looking in here every day just to make sure everything's all right."

Karl shifted his position in his chair.

"I'll be out tomorrow," he whispered, "to help with the cows."

When nobody responded to that empty promise, Kurt could hear the ticking of the wooden schoolhouse clock hanging on the wall opposite the stove.

"Don't worry about helping with the cows," Henry said. "Arny and Kurt and I are doing what needs to be done. We're taking care of everything."

"Reinharts raise hogs and beef cattle," Karl mumbled under his blankets. "Reinharts don't milk cows."

"Edna," Henry said, "showed us what to do the day you took sick. You've got nothing to worry about. We're doing what Edna tells us to do."

Which was what Karl had done when he was still able to do it.

Chapter Eight

The Reverend Crosley had told his congregation there was only one reason Henry Reinhart was so willing to help the Boeckers.

"That scoundrel covets their land," the minister charged from his pulpit one Sunday morning, "and I say there's no telling what he'll do, or the lengths he'll go, to get it."

In the same sermon, Cecil asked for volunteers to do the Boeckers' work for them during Karl's illness. They were to meet in his office after the service. He reminded his congregation it was the Christian thing to do.

Whatever it was, nobody showed up for it.

"Hell," the people said behind Cecil's back, "let those Reinharts do it."

So went the story Elaine and Arny brought back from town with their groceries, a story they shared with Bertha, Henry and Kurt during their supper that evening.

Kurt's grandfather acted unimpressed, as if the news had nothing to do with him. He gave his grandson a brief knowing look, though, after he heard the churchgoers had chosen to defer to the heathen Reinharts when it came time to help their neighbors.

*****

"It's a shame we couldn't have children," Edna Boecker muttered across the table to Kurt as if he and she were alone. "Your grandfather owns a lot of land now, but we've never had more than these eighty acres my mother and father left me."

"Arny says your old milking machine won't last much longer," Henry said. "He's made it do until now, though."

Edna put her hands together in front of her on the table as if she were praying.

It was the same kind of round oak table the Reinharts had in their kitchen, but the surface of the Boeckers' table bore the stains of numerous foods and fluids Kurt's family would've wiped away within moments of their spillage.

"Arny is such a sweet man," Edna said, looking at Henry again. "Bertha told me Elaine does most of the work inside your house."

"She does," Henry said. "She's very helpful. I'm glad Arny

married her."

"I understand," Edna said, "she tends to your chickens, too."

"Kurt helps her with that now," Henry said.

"That's nice," Edna said, glancing at Kurt as if she were flirting with him.

With a sigh, she turned to Henry again.

"Arny and Elaine have been married quite a while now," she said. "Since before the war?"

"It's been that long," Henry said.

"And still no children for them," Edna said. "I assume they've tried."

Kurt could tell from the look on his grandfather's face he wasn't about to respond to those remarks.

"How many cows have gone dry?" Karl Boecker asked.

He was so hoarse Kurt could scarcely understand what he was saying.

"You had half a dozen dry when you got sick," Henry shouted across the room. "We're still milking the other nine."

He looked at Edna.

"But they'll all be dry soon enough," he said, lowering his voice. "You don't have enough corn and hay to feed them."

"What do you intend to do with our herd?" Edna asked. She, unlike Henry, kept her voice loud enough for Karl to hear her. "Send them to the stockyards to be sold and slaughtered? They'll make good bologna, won't they? They're too old for us to be milking them anymore. Isn't that what you're telling me? They're too old for anything except going to the butcher?"

*****

Kurt had recently gone to the stockyards in Chicago with his grandfather. At four o'clock one cold morning between Christmas and New Year's, on a day Kurt didn't have to be in school, Emil Olson came down from Kensington with his semi to pick up a load of hogs.

Kurt sat on the hard leather seat in the cab between Emil and his grandfather.

Kurt guessed Emil was in his fifties. Elaine liked to warn Arny, if he wasn't careful, he'd end up as beefy as Emil Olson was.

He talked in a monotone about some people who'd lost their farms in the Depression.

"That happens," Henry said. "Especially when people don't want to work hard and pay strict attention to where their money's coming from and going to."

Emil guffawed. "Nobody will ever accuse you of anything like that."

Earlier that morning, Henry had objected to Emil's updated pricing schedule, which his new truck supposedly justified. Henry threatened to take all of his livestock-hauling business to a competitor in Edinburgh. Emil backed down and let Henry pay the old price.

Kurt fell asleep leaning against his grandfather's shoulder and didn't wake up again until they were in Chicago and he began to smell the stockyards. The sun, behind a thick haze of coal smoke, was as pale and dim as he'd ever seen it. He couldn't fathom why anyone would choose to live in a city so grim.

After the commission agent sold the hogs that morning and gave Henry his check, Kurt, his grandfather and Emil visited a packinghouse for a free tour and lunch the agent had arranged for them, to show how grateful he was for Henry's business.

They and the other people in their tour group peered through a window into a room filled with hogs—which looked remarkably like the Hampshires Kurt's grandfather had sold.

Two men slipped metal clamps around the hind legs of the animals. Chains lifted the squealing pigs off their feet and conveyed them heads down through a hole in the wall into another room.

The group hurried to the next window, where they could see the overhead conveyor mechanism bring one hog at a time to a large man Emil later referred to as a "darky."

The man worked in a pool of blood reaching halfway up his hip-high rubber boots. Wielding a long knife and turning now and then to the window with a grin on his face, he made an incision across each hog's throat. His cut was so precise the onlookers couldn't tell what he'd done until the animal moved past him and blood began spurting from its fatal wound.

"Pork chops!" the man cried, laughing and waving his knife at Kurt on the other side of the window as if his throat might be next.

Remembering Johnny's imaginary machine gun, Kurt also

laughed.

*****

"We've found a buyer for some of your cows," Henry said. "He owns a big dairy farm near Maple Grove. He'll come and pick them up tomorrow if we get these papers signed and notarized today."

"How many will he take?" Edna asked.

"I'm not sure," Henry replied.

"You know," she countered.

"Two of them, I think, maybe three."

"And the other dozen or thirteen," Edna said, "will soon end up in a packing plant in Chicago."

Kurt's grandfather shrugged his shoulders.

"They're pretty damned old," he said, nodding his head at the man in the corner by the stove. "He didn't keep his herd built up. He sold all his heifers the last few years. You do that very long and you end up with a bunch of old, worn-out cows."

"We sold the calves," Karl mumbled under his blankets, "to buy feed for the cows. That was Edna's idea."

Karl had suffered a stroke the same day Henry and Kurt had gone to the stockyards in Chicago.

After Edna made a tearful plea over the telephone to Bertha, the Reinharts did all the outside work on the Boeckers' farm.

Edna and Bertha had been neighbors from the day Bertha was born. Edna had assisted at her birth.

Edna gave Henry a defiant look.

"We had no choice," she said. "We either sold the calves or got a loan from Chester Smith and mortgaged our farm."

Chapter Nine

Henry sat across the kitchen table from Edna as if he were a president in granite on Mount Rushmore.

"The bank is holding my certified check," he said. "They'll deposit it in your account as soon as you and I call and let them know you and Karl have signed these papers. Their notary will put his seal on the papers when my grandson and I return them to the bank signed by you and Karl. Chester gave me his promise that's how they'll do it."

Chester Smith and his wife, Gwendolyn, owned the Kensington State Bank.

Henry and Kurt had brought the papers down from Kensington. Karl and Edna Boecker were a generation older than Henry. And he was in their house with his grandson that afternoon to buy their farm.

Edna removed her reading glasses from her apron pocket and maneuvered them with both hands so they rested on her ears and nose where they helped her the most. She stared at the papers Henry had brought her to sign.

"So it's thirty-six thousand dollars?" she asked.

"It's thirty-six thousand," Henry said. "That's four hundred fifty dollars an acre. There's a bank receipt in there with those papers."

"It won't do me any good to look at your papers," Edna said, peering over her glasses at Henry. "You know I can't read. I'll have to take your word for it. If you cheat Karl and me, there isn't anything I can do about it. I'm alone now. I'm at your mercy."

Edna and Karl Boecker hadn't gotten any help from the Reverend Cecil Crosley. And they'd attended his church almost every Sunday from the day his father had opened it in Kensington. Their offerings were said to be generous.

Henry Reinhart, on the other hand, would pay them thirty-six thousand dollars for their farm. He'd also agree, in the papers Edna said she couldn't read, to let them both remain in their home until the day they died. Karl had lived in it since he married Edna more than sixty years ago. Edna had never lived anywhere else.

Edna nodded toward her husband in the corner. He was sleeping again.

"He's no good for anything anymore," she said. "I'm at your mercy, Henry."

"Everything's been done properly," Henry said. "Just call the bank and ask Chester if you've got any questions. He had his own lawyers in Edinburgh draw up these documents."

Edna looked down at the neat pile of papers on the table in front of her.

"To tell you the truth," she said, "thirty-six thousand dollars isn't much for a farm."

"Nobody else will pay you that kind of money for it," Henry said. "Chester told you so himself. Nobody else will pay you a penny over three fifty an acre. That's only twenty-eight thousand dollars for your farm."

"We spent our lives here," Edna said, pointing toward the corner again. "Him and me."

"And I'm the only person in the world," Henry said, "who'll pay you for that."

Edna sneered at her adversary. "You're paying eight thousand dollars for our lives? Is that supposed to be four thousand each?"

Kurt knew his grandfather would call those remarks examples of the "phony sentimentality" he had no use for.

"And nobody else," Henry said, "would let you and Karl stay in this house without paying rent for the rest of your lives."

Edna scoffed. "That part of your agreement doesn't amount to much, and you know it. We won't be here much longer."

Henry scoffed himself. "That's ridiculous. I don't know how much longer you'll be here. And neither do you."

Edna picked up the papers and held them in front of her. She peered at the first page for a long time, almost as if she were reading it.

Kurt glanced at Karl and quickly took another look. Had Karl stopped breathing?

The fire was down, and the air in the kitchen had turned colder again.

Edna put the top page at the bottom of the pile and pretended to read the second page as carefully as she had the first.

When it became apparent to Kurt that Edna was going to peruse each paper in the pile in that manner, he looked once more at Karl, who lay under his blankets as motionless as a corpse in a coffin.

Kurt struggled against his worst thoughts as if they were tears. Had Karl Boecker died?

Kurt tried to reassure himself nothing was wrong. Still, he couldn't pry his eyes off Karl.

"Does it really say in these papers," Edna asked, "we can live in this house for the rest of our lives?"

"The lawyers put that in there," Kurt's grandfather replied. "Chester can confirm they did. He read all those papers. He knows what's in them and what isn't. He's in the bank right now. Why don't you call him? You know the number."

"Chester Smith," Edna said, not taking her eyes off the page she held in front of her, "knows everybody's business, whether they want him to or not. I'll have to trust you, Henry Reinhart. As I said, I'm at your mercy."

*****

The temperature that day didn't rise above zero, even though the sun was shining in a clear blue sky, and the foot of new snow from the day before was too bright to look at directly.

In Edna and Karl Boecker's kitchen, though, it was dark. The insides of their windows were covered with frost. The one working bulb in a three-bulb ceiling fixture provided the only light in the room.

Kurt could no longer hear any fire in the stove, only the dreadful, insistent ticking of the clock on the wall. To him, the situation had become as absurd as the worst of his dreams—in which his father, the man they'd called Johnny, took him up to his grandfather's house on the hill to die with him, and Kurt's grandfather let him do it.

Karl, slumped in his chair in the corner, was dying, or was already dead. Edna had claimed she couldn't read the papers, but she held them in front of her anyway and studied them as if they told her a story she couldn't put down.

Kurt wanted to say something to his grandfather about Karl.

Instead, letting the nightmare unfold, he said and did nothing.

*****

Edna Boecker laid the papers back down on the table.

Kurt glanced away from Karl long enough to see the page on top of the pile had been in that position when Edna first picked the papers up.

"So," she said, looking at Kurt's grandfather, "it comes down to this. You won't help us with the cows when spring comes again."

"We can't," Henry replied. "We've got four hundred and eighty acres to work and cattle and hogs to feed. We won't have enough time to take care of your cows. I'm sorry."

A crooked smile broke across Edna's face like a slow bolt of lightning.

"And yet you want another eighty acres to work," she said. "You and your family will find the time to do that."

"We will," Kurt said, knowing he was speaking out of turn.

Henry nodded toward his grandson. "This boy helps us the most in the summer months when we've got the biggest share of our work to do. He knows it'll take us much less time to work your eighty acres along with ours than it would to milk your cows morning and night. And we'll make more off your eighty acres than you do. He understands that, too."

"You'll rip out our fences," Edna said, "and tear down our barns."

"We can use your corncrib," Henry said. "We'll keep that. Your dairy barn is ready to fall down by itself without any help from us. The fences will just be in our way."

"But it's written in these lawyers' papers, isn't it, you've got to leave this house standing as long as either of us is still alive?"

"That's what it says in those papers."

"Chester Smith told you we're down to nothing."

"He didn't have to tell me that," Henry said. "Any fool can see you don't have enough from your milk check to get you through the month. You don't have the money to buy wood or coal. So you've got nothing to burn in your stove but corncobs. Which you should've ground up with your corn to feed your cows."

"We didn't have enough money," Edna said, "to pay Larson to do that."

*****

Eric Larson was one of five sons of tenant farmers. After he graduated from high school in 1948, he joined the army and spent the last year of his enlistment fighting in Korea. When he returned to Lafayette County in 1951, he used the money he'd sent home each month to make a down payment on a feed-grinding truck.

The farmers who hired Eric to grind their corn and oats into feed for their livestock didn't have to buy and install expensive equipment of their own to get the job done. The machinery would mostly remain idle and therefore not produce, as Henry would say, a sufficient return on the money they'd invested in it.

Eric, dark haired despite his last name, did a lot of work for Kurt's grandfather, almost all of it late in the afternoon or on Saturdays when Kurt was home from school and could help. Arny, who detested the dust grinding corn and oats raised, was grateful he didn't need to be Eric's helper. Kurt, ignoring the dirt and drudgery, focused his thoughts on Eric, whose optimism and amusing remarks made the work seem like a game two friends could play forever.

Chapter Ten

Henry had waited more than forty years for the chance to buy Edna's eighty acres.

"I can see what's going on here," he said. "I haven't noticed any smoke from your furnace chimney for at least two weeks. You're only using your kitchen stove for heat. You and Karl must sleep in your chairs in this room, buried under your blankets."

"You know more about us," Edna said, "than Chester Smith, Cecil Crosley and Albert Rauenthaler put together."

"I wouldn't claim to know more about anything than those people do," Henry said. "But unlike them, I'm willing to help you."

"Nobody will help us," she said. "You know it. I know it. There isn't anything we can do now but sell our farm to you, Henry Reinhart."

She looked at her opponent—the person the Reverend Crosley claimed was an agent of Satan himself—and grimaced.

"And that's the one thing," she said, "we promised ourselves we'd never do."

*****

Edna Boecker opened her blankets for a moment and produced a fountain pen from the pocket of her apron. She arched an eyebrow in the direction of Kurt's grandfather.

"When did you say," she asked, "the cows go?"

"We'll milk them tonight," Henry replied, "and again in the morning. And tomorrow they all go."

"Tomorrow they all go," Edna repeated. "I won't miss them. They've been nothing but trouble for a long time. Milking them didn't get Karl and me anywhere. We should've raised beef cattle and hogs the way you Reinharts do. Here we are at the end of our lives, and we don't have anything to show for what we did. No children. No grandchildren. No farm. Those damned cows ate it right out from under us. We haven't got anything worth having."

The look on Henry's face was as hard and cold as the frost on the windows.

"You'll soon have thirty-six thousand dollars in your bank account," he said.

Kurt looked at Edna and saw that crooked smile again.

"All a bank account is good for," she said, "is to make sure they send the doctor, the groceries and the coal. And they bury us right, with Christian funerals and graves."

Kurt couldn't bear to peek at Karl again, but he did.

This time he was certain the man was dead.

"Any bank account," Kurt heard his grandfather say, "is better than nothing. And a bank account with thirty-six thousand dollars in it is a hell of a lot better than nothing."

Edna looked down at the documents on the table in front of her.

"You just tell me, Henry Reinhart, where to sign your papers."

*****

Kurt stood next to Edna, pointing out the lines provided for her signature, watching her draw the letters of her name with the care and solemnity of a child new to cursive.

The kitchen had become so cold Kurt had put his gloves on. Nobody needed his signature.

His grandfather had shown him the bin off the side of the back porch, where the Boeckers kept whatever they burned in their kitchen stove. He said they didn't have enough corncobs left to fight the cold beyond the next afternoon. After that, they'd freeze to death.

Edna finished signing the papers, laid her pen on the table and looked at her husband.

"My God!" she said. "We took too long!"

Kurt's grandfather, startled, looked where Edna was looking.

"Is he all right?" he asked.

"If he's dead," Edna replied, getting up from her chair and limping over to Karl's, "we'll have to ask Chester Smith and those lawyers what to do. I suppose it was my mistake long ago putting his name on the deed. I thought that's the way married people should own a farm, jointly. But maybe, if he's already dead, we won't need his signature. Isn't that what joint ownership is all about?"

Edna's remarks failed to amuse Kurt or his grandfather, who stood on either side of Karl attempting to detect signs of life.

Edna placed her hands on her husband's shoulders and shook him with more force than Kurt would've thought it possible for her to muster.

Karl didn't respond.

"The farm, Henry Reinhart," Edna said, "is yours."

Kurt realized he should've said something to his grandfather and Edna about Karl.

"Wake up!" Edna yelled at her husband. "Wake up!"

She pushed and pulled his shoulders.

Kurt held back his tears until he saw what he most wanted to see. Karl slowly opened his eyes.

"That's good," Edna said. "That's more like it."

Karl was in a stupor. He sat in his chair looking up at the three people hovering over him as if he'd never seen them before.

"You've got to sit up straight now and do some work," Edna said. "You've got to sign some papers. We're selling our farm to Henry Reinhart. We'll be rich. We'll have thirty-six thousand dollars in Chester Smith's bank up in Kensington. The first thing we'll do, we'll get us some coal. We'll burn it in the furnace and warm up the whole damned house again."

"They'll deliver it by suppertime," Henry said. "Elaine talked to them."

When Edna had her husband sitting up as much as he could, she pulled from under his chair a *Life* magazine. She placed it on Karl's lap. She soon had her right hand around his, holding her pen.

Kurt, seeing what she meant to do, went to the table, brought back the pages Karl needed to sign, and laid the first one on the magazine.

As Kurt and his grandfather watched, Edna drew her husband's signature where it needed to be.

Kurt and Edna repeated the process for all the pages.

When they were finished, she removed the magazine and wrapped Karl in his blankets again.

"You can go back to sleep now," she said to him. "Your work is done."

*****

On their way home from Kensington in his grandfather's 1936 Pontiac, Kurt was glad they didn't have far to go. The heater in the old car provided little more warmth than the corncobs in the Boeckers' kitchen stove had. But he doubted the frigid air alone, after such a victory, could account for the grim look he saw on his grandfather's face.

"Can they stay there the rest of their lives?" Kurt asked. "Do those papers really say that?"

His grandfather stared ahead at the road through the small hole the inefficient defroster had made at the bottom of the windshield.

"Isn't that what I told her?" Henry asked his nine-year-old grandson.

The wind was blowing the previous day's snow over the road.

"The Boeckers will be in that house another twenty years," Henry said. "At least Edna will. She'll be there when I'm dead. That was the worst deal I've ever made. Thirty-six thousand dollars for eighty goddamned acres. I must be out of my mind."

Kurt peered through the hole at the bottom of his side of the windshield.

"You could've put anything you wanted in those papers," he said. "Edna claims she can't read. Karl never even looked at them."

Henry shook his head, but the expression on his face remained unchanged. "Edna Boecker can read. She never went to school, and she's always said she can't read, but that doesn't mean she's telling the truth. You suppose she just looks at the pictures in those newspapers and magazines they've got lying around there? Karl can read but not very well. But Edna can read just as well as I can. She taught herself how to do it. My father sent me to school. I'm grateful he did. I believe in reading. That was the main difference between my father's older children and me. They never learned to read or write, German or English. My father could read and write both. So can Edna."

Henry had to scrunch down in his seat and look through the steering wheel in order to see the road in front of them.

"Edna read every word on every page," he said. "That's why she took so damned long. You can't put anything over on her. I told Chester Smith's lawyers to be extra careful to include in those papers every little thing she wanted. If she'd thought I'd left anything out, it would've queered the deal. No, every word in that stack of papers was on the up-and-up."

The car plowed through the drifts of snow with a bucking thump, thump, thump, like a ship—Captain Ahab's, Kurt imagined—under full sail before the wind.

"Hell," Henry said, "I have to admit to you, Edna Boecker took me. She's probably sitting there in her kitchen right now laughing at me."

Kurt couldn't imagine Edna sitting in her kitchen laughing at anybody.

Kurt's grandfather, gripping the wheel with his bare, gnarled hands, was silent the rest of the way home.

Kurt, though, couldn't help but ask his grandfather one more question.

"How do you intend to get Albert Rauenthaler's farm?"

"I'll get it," Henry said. "Maybe not tomorrow. But I'll get it."

Chapter Eleven

K arl Boecker died the first morning after the day he and Edna sold their farm. For one night only, he'd enjoyed the warmth of coal burning in their furnace again.

Edna lived alone in the house through one more spring and summer.

Then one day the next September, soon after the hickories began turning yellow, Arny found her sitting at her kitchen table with her chin on her bosom as if she were sleeping.

He could tell, though, from the stiffness of her body, she was dead.

*****

The Boeckers had no close family members still alive or any distant relatives who'd maintained contact with them.

They therefore had to choose who should receive whatever money was left in their bank account when they died.

Karl had wanted to leave everything to the Kensington Christian Church.

"It would be proof," he'd said, according to the story Edna told Bertha, "of our faith in a Christian God."

Edna, though, decided not to do that.

When it had become known, even before Karl died, that he and Edna might sell their farm to Henry Reinhart, Reverend Crosley made reference in several of his Sunday sermons, without unnecessarily naming names, to deals made with the devil.

Kensington was therefore curious to find out who'd end up with the money Henry had paid the Boeckers for their farm, almost all of which was still said to be in their account at the Kensington State Bank on the day Edna died.

After the lawyers filed Edna's will in probate court, the truth came out in the *Edinburgh Times*. She'd left the money to the Edinburgh Community Hospital.

"Why?" was the universal question.

Neither Karl nor Edna had spent a day in any hospital.

Within a week, another, lengthier article on the subject appeared on the front page of the *Times*. The Edinburgh Community Hospital wasn't a charitable organization. It was a for-profit business corporation.

Two of its three shareholders, each owning a third of the shares, were doctors who treated their patients in the hospital. The third shareholder was the president of the Kensington State Bank, Chester Smith.

The doctors and Chester, the story went on, had given the *Times* a statement.

"We solemnly promise," they said, "we'll use the Edna Boecker bequest to make improvements to the hospital strictly for the benefit of its patients, and not in any way, shape or form for ourselves. A committee of lawyers has agreed to oversee disbursements from the bequest to make absolutely certain none of it ends up in the hands of the shareholders."

The overseers included the lawyers, Kurt noticed, who'd drawn up the legal papers Edna and Karl signed that cold February afternoon in their kitchen.

The statement also failed to explain how any improvements to the hospital wouldn't benefit its shareholders.

*****

At the Reinharts' supper table the autumn Thursday the story of Edna Boecker's will appeared in the paper, Elaine and Arny dared to speak of it.

Bertha said she felt deeply sorry Chester Smith, the doctors and their lawyers had so easily hoodwinked her old friend, Edna.

After supper, Henry read the article at the kitchen table while Kurt tried to do his homework.

Arny, Elaine and Bertha were sitting on the sofa in the living room making use of the television set Henry had reluctantly given them the money to buy.

After he finished reading the article, he rolled up the paper and slapped it on the table so hard the sound startled the Reinharts two rooms away viewing *Dragnet*.

Kurt, who'd earlier read the story, was waiting for his grandfather's response to it.

"You and I," Henry said to his grandson, "are going to see Chester Smith."

His Grandfather's House

*****

Two mornings later, a Saturday, it was raining when Kurt woke. They wouldn't pick corn that day.

Elaine and Arny were already laughing at their good fortune. They'd do the work Henry expected of them, but they'd have plenty of time for television, too.

During morning chores, Henry told Kurt they'd also take advantage of the weather.

"We'll go to Kensington and have a talk," he said, "with the most conniving crook who's ever breathed air on this planet."

*****

Henry and Kurt sat in two leather chairs across a mahogany desk from Chester Smith.

It was by far the largest desk Kurt had seen. Neat stacks of documents, reminding him of the pile the Boeckers had signed, lay on it in a grid, like sections in a township.

"I know what this is all about," Chester said, glaring at Henry. "But don't you think your grandson is a bit too young to hear what you and I might have to say?"

Whereas Elaine, with her nose and eyes, made Kurt think of an eagle, middle-aged Chester, with his, was an owl.

"Hell no, he isn't," Henry replied. "His teachers have yet to give him anything but an A on his report cards."

Chester looked at Kurt with a thin-lipped smile.

"What grade are you in?" he asked. "Do you like school?"

"I'm in fifth grade," Kurt replied. "I like school a lot, but it's too slow."

"Too slow?" Chester asked with a puzzled expression on his face.

"He thinks," Kurt's grandfather said, "he should be doing what they do in high school. He's read through all the grade school books. He's going through the high school trigonometry book now, and he tells me he understands it. I believe he does, too."

"I see," Chester said, turning back to Henry. "Now what can I do for you?"

Kurt assumed Chester didn't want a witness present, but his grandfather did.

*****

"I won't beat around the bush," Henry said. "I've come here for my eight thousand dollars."

Chester glanced at Kurt as if he might still have a question or two about the propriety of the boy's presence in his office. But then he merely shrugged his shoulders and resumed his icy glare at Henry.

"Your eight thousand dollars?" he asked.

"The Boecker farm," Henry began, "was worth twenty-eight thousand dollars. You and your crooked doctor and lawyer friends can have that. You don't deserve a penny of it, but I couldn't care less whether you get it or not. If your crowd hadn't taken that money off those old fools, some other bunch of crooks would've."

Chester smiled at that as if Henry had praised him.

"But the eight thousand extra I paid for their farm," Henry continued. "That's another matter. I'll be goddamned if I'll sit back and let you steal it from me."

Chester smirked again. "I don't know what you're talking about. You paid thirty-six thousand for Edna and Karl's farm. They saw fit to leave it to that fine hospital we have in Edinburgh. Some people say it's the best hospital in the state outside of Chicago. I don't know why you think anybody owes you any money. You have the eighty acres you wanted so much you were willing to place a bid nobody else would even consider matching. That's what you paid eight thousand dollars for, Henry—your vanity."

"Then here's what we'll do," Henry said. "Have your people write a check to me for every cent I have in this bank at this moment, interest included. I called the people at the bank in Edinburgh. It's got ten times the assets your bank has. And their interest rates are just as good as yours. My grandson confirmed that. They said they'd stay open today as long as needed for me to bring them your check. I'll be doing business with them from now on."

Through the window behind Chester, Kurt could see the rain hadn't let up.

Chester stared at Henry. "I'll have my employees prepare a check for you for four thousand dollars. The lawyers will say it's a settlement of a potential lawsuit that could never prevail but would cost the bank that much to get rid of. I'll have someone call the bank in Edinburgh and let them know they can close as early today as they wish."

"Bring the check," Henry said. "Let me see it. And then have one of your employees make that call."

Chester looked at Kurt and laughed.

"It's all arithmetic," he said. "I got A's in that, too. My father was proud of me."

*****

After Henry deposited the check in one of his and Bertha's accounts at the Kensington State Bank, he drove home in the rain with Kurt.

"Liars, crooks and thieves," Henry mumbled. "See how this world is?"

Kurt saw how it was. He also saw his grandfather doing business with liars, crooks and thieves and making no apology for it.

Chapter Twelve

When Edna and Karl Boecker gave up the struggle and sold their farm to Henry Reinhart in 1953, Albert Rauenthaler's eighty acres were the only part of the section Kurt's grandfather didn't own.

One Saturday morning that autumn, after the Reinharts had finished picking their corn, ten-year-old Kurt learned how Albert viewed his grandfather's designs on his land.

Kurt came out of the bakery in Kensington with the bag of sweet rolls Elaine and Arny had asked him to buy for them. Kurt and his grandfather didn't eat what Henry called "teeth-rotting" sweet rolls.

If Kurt had seen Albert approaching him on the sidewalk—if Kurt hadn't been watching Eric Larson drive his truck through town with his current girlfriend in the passenger seat as if they were in a parade—he would've crossed to the other side of the street.

But here the large man was, in front of him, blocking his way, staring down at him.

Albert, who was in his late seventies then, wagged his finger in Kurt's face.

"Don't look at me like that," Albert said. "I can promise you your granddad will never get my land. And that's what he wants more than anything else in this world."

Taking note of the frightened look on Kurt's face, Albert laughed.

The people on Main Street ceased whatever they were doing and stared at Albert and Kurt. Eric, fearing Albert meant to attack Kurt physically, stopped his truck, jumped out of it and came running.

"Go home now!" Albert continued, loud enough for all the onlookers to hear. "Go home and tell that granddad of yours he'll never get my land! I'll be the one to stop him!"

Eric threw his right arm around Kurt's shoulders and walked between him and Albert.

"You got yourself a crew cut," Eric said to Kurt.

Kurt had done it only because Eric had. He'd even gone to Eric's barber to get it.

They reached Elaine and Arny, who stood beside Henry's 1936 Pontiac parked on Main Street. They held their brown paper bags of groceries in their arms as speechless and motionless as figures in a painting celebrating the common man and woman.

Kurt turned to Eric and laughed. "Thank you for saving me from Albert."

After Eric gave Kurt a hug and ran back to his truck and girlfriend, Kurt held up the white paper bag of sweet rolls in front of his aunt and uncle and brought them back to life.

*****

On a Tuesday evening toward the end of the next winter, in 1954, Arny, Elaine and Bertha sat watching Milton Berle perform in drag when Bertha said she felt dizzy.

Arny and Elaine helped her to bed. Kurt followed them up the stairs and convinced his aunt and uncle they shouldn't deny themselves the pleasure of watching Berle's antics. He remained with his grandmother until she fell asleep.

When Bertha, who was seventy-two, chose not to get out of bed the next morning, the other Reinharts assumed she had a cold.

As the days passed into a week and she still didn't want to get up from her bed, Arny began to insist they take her to a hospital, or at least to a doctor.

Kurt's grandfather, though, scoffed at the idea and made it clear he didn't think such drastic measures were required for a cold or a touch of the flu or whatever it was Bertha had. He also thought the rest was helping her. Elaine agreed with him. So did Kurt.

Bertha herself wasn't in favor of Arny's proposal. She told Kurt she had no wish to go anywhere. She'd be fine, she assured him, just where she was.

Whenever Kurt was in the house, he took his grandmother her meals and whatever else she wanted.

Then she woke up one day and complained the dizziness had come back and she could scarcely breathe.

As the morning wore on, Arny demanded, with increasing vehemence, they take her to a doctor. In the early afternoon, without asking his mother or father for their permission, he called a doctor and began describing his mother's symptoms.

The doctor cut him off and told him to take his mother to the hospital in Edinburgh immediately. The doctor would meet them there.

Bertha, though, wanted to stay where she was—in her own bed.

His Grandfather's House

Henry agreed with her, contending this was just another doctor's attempt to grab their money. Arny had in fact called one of the two doctors who owned the hospital with Smith.

As Henry and Arny continued to argue over the supper table, Kurt came down from upstairs with news that silenced them. Bertha had died.

*****

When Kurt called his fifth-grade teacher, she told him he should stay home as long as he wished. She was certain he could make up later whatever tests he'd miss during his absence.

The next morning Kurt went with his grandfather and uncle up to his great-grandfather's orchard to dig a grave for his grandmother.

After Henry and Kurt took measurements with a yardstick, outlined the proposed grave with two-by-fours and began digging, Arny threw down his spade as if it were a weapon he couldn't bring himself to use.

At first, Henry paid no attention to him.

Then Arny stood in front of his father and forced him to stop digging and look at him.

"It wouldn't cost you much," Arny said, "to pay the Gibsons to come up here with their digger and do this. They told me on the phone they'd charge you a hundred dollars. They said they told you the same thing."

"Why should I throw away that kind of money?" Henry asked. "We'll be done with this job in no time, and we can get back to doing some useful work. Now get out of my way."

Arny stepped backwards over one of the two-by-fours.

His father resumed digging.

"That boy," he said, nodding toward Kurt, "will dig a lot more dirt today than you will."

Approaching his eleventh birthday, Kurt was growing rapidly. So much so the aggressive older boys at school—those who smoked cigarettes, drank alcohol and made every attempt they could to give their female classmates a "feel," as they called it—had given up trying to pick a fight with him.

"What's the matter with you?" Henry asked Arny. "You helped

dig your brother's grave. You didn't complain about that."

"We had to dig his by hand," Arny said. "Nobody around here had a digger then."

"Progress," Kurt's grandfather sneered, "doesn't mean we have to pay for things we can easily do ourselves."

"It wouldn't hurt you to pay for it," Arny said, his voice breaking. "For her."

"For her? For Bertha?" Henry asked. "There isn't anything anybody can do for her now. She's dead."

After Arny composed himself, he tried again.

"I don't like doing this," he said. "Knowing it's for her. I don't like thinking about digging a hole in the ground and putting her it."

Kurt kept working and said nothing.

"Everybody," Henry said, "ends up in a hole like this. What goddamned difference does it make how it gets dug?"

Arny wiped his shirtsleeve across his face, but he wouldn't give up.

"You talk about her," he said, "as if she were just another person who needed to be buried."

Continuing to dig Bertha's grave was Henry's only response to that.

"It isn't surprising," Arny said to his father, his voice quavering, "people say you murdered your brother and cheated him and your sisters out of your father's farm."

Kurt stopped digging and looked at his uncle.

Henry kept digging.

"You listen to a lot of idiotic gossip," he said. "I assume it entertains you—like that stupid stuff you watch on that box."

Henry emptied his spade on the mound of earth he and Kurt had begun building next to the grave.

"But I'll be goddamned," he said, looking at Arny, "if I ever expected you'd repeat those lies to me."

Arny remained silent.

"We don't need you up here anymore," Henry said. "Kurt and I can finish this job by ourselves. Go down to the house and find something useful to do. Help Elaine with whatever she's doing. She knows what needs to be done."

Arny looked through his tears at his father, who had more to say.

His Grandfather's House

"You thought dragging your mother to a hospital against her wishes would do her any good. Don't you realize how wrong you were? Can't you see how much she didn't want that? I gave her what she wanted. She died in her own bed in the house she always considered her home. She died with her grandson by her bed, at her side. That's what she wanted. I could see she did. Why couldn't you?"

Arny, still in tears, walked away from his mother's grave site and his father's disdain.

Bertha had died listening to Henry and Arny, downstairs at the supper table in the kitchen, arguing about what they should do with her.

She'd looked at Kurt, who was kneeling on the floor next to her bed. She took his hands in hers, gave him a flickering smile—and let herself go.

Chapter Thirteen

As Arny, sobbing, disappeared down the hill on the other side of the orchard, Kurt glanced at the row of seven headstones marking the graves of his ancestors.

The first two were for Otto's wives.

Emma Schaefer Reinhart
b. Dec. 16, 1821
m. Otto Wilhelm Reinhart Feb. 4, 1839
d. Jan. 5, 1887

Anna Bauer Reinhart
b. June 21, 1852
m. Otto Wilhelm Reinhart July 20, 1887
d. May 4, 1888

Kurt knew the day of Anna's death was also the day she gave birth to his grandfather.

Although more than a generation separated Otto Reinhart's two wives, they'd lain together in his orchard, side by side, just the two of them, for another generation before he joined them. The third headstone was his.

Otto Wilhelm Reinhart
b. Jan. 10, 1820
m. Emma Schaefer Reinhart Feb. 4, 1839
m. Anna Bauer Reinhart July 20, 1887
d. Feb. 24, 1911

Otto and his first wife, Emma, had three children. None of them married or had children. Their stones came next.

Conrad Wilhelm Reinhart
b. Feb. 17, 1855
d. Mar. 3, 1912

Lena Frieda Reinhart
b. Dec. 21, 1840
d. Dec. 15, 1921

Cora Emma Reinhart
b. Nov. 8, 1839
d. Jan. 10, 1922

Kurt lingered a bit, staring at the seventh stone.

John Henry Reinhart
b. Oct. 23, 1924
m. Lorelei Juergen Reinhart Dec. 24, 1942
d. May 17, 1947

*****

After Kurt and his grandfather finished digging Bertha's grave, they gathered up their spades and Arny's and the two-by-fours and began the walk to the toolshed next to the barn.

Henry paused when they reached the house Otto had built and lived in during most of his seventy-five years in America.

"From now on," Henry said, looking at the house, "you and I will live here."

The older children in that part of Lafayette County told their younger siblings and neighbors the Reinharts' vacant house on the hill was haunted. The existence of a cemetery up there, where they buried Johnny, proved it. Kurt's classmates had all heard the story.

When Henry and Kurt entered the kitchen in the house down by the road, Arny and Elaine were sitting at the table drinking coffee with their latest bag of sweet rolls from the bakery in Kensington.

Arny stared down at the table with one hand to his forehead as if he might be deep in thought. His eyes, though, were red from crying. His chin trembled.

Kurt's grandfather came right to the point. "You won't have to worry about your mean old father anymore. Kurt and I are moving out of here. This was your mother's house. It was never mine. I lived in it solely to please her."

Kurt and Elaine looked at one another.

Kurt often felt it made a difference to Elaine that he was Johnny and Lorelei's son and not Arny and hers. And yet he couldn't say she'd ever been unkind to him.

She'd gone along with his refusal to eat the food the school served in its cafeteria. She helped him prepare lunches from home until he was old enough to do it by himself.

Arny removed his hand from his face.

Elaine set her cup down on her saucer.

"Kurt and I," Henry announced, "are moving into my father's house. I'll have the electricians and plumbers come here as soon as they can. I'll pay them extra to work overtime and on the weekend."

The plumbers and electricians would both be starting out from scratch on this project.

Once again, Arny and Elaine looked at one another.

"Now that Bertha's gone," Henry said, "I want nothing more to do with this house. You two can have it. You can live here by yourselves. But my grandson comes with me."

*****

Arny insisted upon a funeral service for his mother. Kurt and Elaine decided to go with him. The last time Kurt had been in the Kensington Christian Church was for Johnny's funeral.

Kurt thought the church would be empty. His grandmother had no relatives other than her spouse, son, daughter-in-law and grandson. The only friends she could've claimed, Edna and Karl Boecker, had predeceased her.

When Arny, Elaine and Kurt entered the church, though, they found it as full as it had been for Johnny's funeral. When they reached the first-row center pew reserved for them, Chester Smith himself rose from his second-row seat to whisper his condolences.

Arny and Elaine shook his hand. Kurt ignored him.

But he welcomed the hug Chester's wife, Gwendolyn, gave him. She'd gone out of her way to speak with him whenever she saw him in Kensington. He thought the schoolteachers in her book club might've had something to do with that.

People who knew slender, auburn-haired Gwendolyn in high school in the 1920s agreed she still looked much as she had then. Kurt assumed she'd married Chester for his family's money and position in the community and not because she loved him.

In his sermon, Reverend Crosley, now well into his seventies and stooped a bit, first addressed the character and earthly activities of the deceased. It required a thorough discussion of the possible willingness of a forgiving God to welcome into His ultimate fold a person who'd amply demonstrated she was a half-hearted believer at best.

The day Bertha died she'd surprised Kurt. She told him she'd come to doubt everything Cecil had said. She did hope, though, she and Kurt would be reunited with their family again in some kind of afterlife. Maybe even Johnny and Lorelei would be there.

"We must always understand, however," Reverend Crosley continued, moving into the second and far more important part of his sermon, "the representatives of the devil who dwell among us and do his work aren't powerless. No."

Cecil saw Kurt shaking his head and glared at him.

"We must understand," he said, "Satan's agents on this earth aren't unlike the most savage beasts in the jungle. We rightly fear them more than we fear death itself. They seek out and prey upon, as if for their sustenance, those of God's children among us who are the weakest, most helpless and most uncertain in their faith. And I say this sort of thing has happened in our community. I say there are those, present in this church today, who are under the dominion of the darkest possible representative of the evil one."

Kurt decided Cecil's entertainment had gone on long enough for him. He stood up.

"My uncle paid you for a funeral service for my grandmother," he said, loud enough for everybody in the church to hear. "But the only thing coming out of your mouth, Cecil, is bullshit. You of all people have no right to sit in judgment on my grandmother and grandfather. You take money for your phony show from people who'd be much better off spending it on their families."

"That's God's money, son!" Cecil shot back.

"God's money?" Kurt asked. "Everybody knows you spend every dime of it on yourself. Too bad you won't be able to take it with you when you go to hell."

As Kurt strode up the aisle to the door, he wiped away his tears.

He'd given the stunned crowd more than what they'd come for.

They cackled, he thought, like the witches in *Macbeth*.

"Did you hear that boy?" he heard one mourner ask.

"He told a Christian minister to his face," another said, "he'll go to hell."

A third laughed. "He's probably right, too."

*****

Leaving the church, Kurt set his sights on the hill in the distance the neighbors called Mount Reinhart.

Crossing one field of March mud after the other, climbing over fences of woven and barbed wire, he walked in a straight line, the most direct route, the shortest path, toward the old house his grandfather had promised him would soon be their home.

A high school student Kurt often sat next to on the bus had given him her copy of *Macbeth* after he'd attended the drama club's production of it. She'd played Lady Macbeth, delivering her line, "What's done, is done," to Lord Macbeth as if he were a child. It was far too late for them to worry about right or wrong.

Kurt went on to read Shakespeare's other tragedies and wondered if those stories might prove to be his own. Would he someday make a life-changing decision only to see it go awry? Would his downfall be as dreadful as those the poet had imagined for Macbeth, Hamlet and Lear?

Part Two

Kurt, Eleven to Fifteen

1954-1958

Chapter Fourteen

After Kurt and his grandfather moved into the house on the hill, they spent their evenings between supper and bedtime at the table in what used to be the dining room.

At Henry's end, on the table and the buffet behind him, were neat stacks of account books, newspapers, business letters, bank statements, deeds, tax returns and plat maps.

Kurt's end was no less occupied or organized. He'd reserved his space on the table for the books and magazines he was currently reading. He'd filled the china cabinet behind him with an encyclopedia, dictionary, atlas of the world, paperback novels and heftier volumes such as the plays and sonnets of Shakespeare and selected works of the English romantic poets.

Otto had handcrafted the three pieces of dining room furniture out of fallen oak.

Kurt and his grandfather did their reading, homework and account keeping beneath three bare bulbs in a chrome ceiling fixture Henry had picked out for the electricians to install. The light glared down on them like the midday summer sun in the fields.

*****

At that table one evening soon after Kurt turned eleven, he summoned the courage to ask his grandfather if he'd murdered his brother.

Henry looked up from his newspaper and stared at his grandson.

"I did not murder my brother," he replied, his voice unwavering.

"What happened that day?" Kurt asked.

"Haven't Arny and Elaine told you the story?"

"They have. But they weren't there. All they can tell me are the stories other people have told them. Those people weren't there either. I want to hear the story from you."

Henry laid his *Tribune* on the table in front of him.

"We got a big rain starting on the first of March that year," he said. "I never saw the creek rise so high before. It was still frozen solid when the storm began. The ice floating in the flood took out the fences crossing the creek on both the east and west sides of the farm. All our livestock were still in the barn then, but we knew we'd have to replace a lot of fence before we turned them loose in the spring."

The Reinharts' livestock roamed the wooded slopes on either side of the creek during the spring, summer and fall.

"The morning after the rain stopped," Henry said, "we could tell the creek had risen as high as it would. Conrad decided we should go down there and figure out how much new fence we'd need to buy so we'd be ready to rebuild it as soon as we could. I was surprised. I'd assumed I'd have to do that on my own. He got down to the creek before I did. He went too close to it, slipped on the mud, fell into the water and got caught in a strong current. After that, he had no chance of survival. He was hungover pretty bad that morning. He was fifty-seven years old. He couldn't swim. All I could do was go to Kensington and call the sheriff. We didn't have a phone then. A deputy found his dead body washed up on a bank of the creek downstream."

"You didn't make any attempt to get him out?"

"I couldn't swim either. If I'd gone into that water, it would've been suicide."

"Grandma told me she saw you running up to your house that morning. She said you appeared to be soaked."

Henry scoffed. "She imagined that. Did she tell you where she was when she saw me?"

"Down by her father's barn."

"You know where that was. How could she tell from there whether I was soaked or not?"

"She thought you'd tried to save Conrad, despite what you told people."

"I made no attempt to save that man."

"Why have only two people in the world, Grandma and me," Kurt asked, "believed you didn't murder your brother?"

"I ended up with the farm, so I must've murdered my brother to get it. My father wasn't supposed to give me the farm in his will and leave nothing to his three children by his first wife. It didn't matter how uneducated they were or how badly the booze had addled their brains. But to tell you the truth, I don't give a good goddamn what other people thought then or what they think now. I know what happened. I didn't murder my brother. My father legally gave me his farm in his will because my brother and sisters would've lost it. That's all that matters to me."

His Grandfather's House

*****

Several weeks after Henry told Kurt his version of the story of his brother Conrad's drowning death, a sudden rainstorm drenched the livestock as they ambled up from the creek to the barn for their evening feed.

Kurt positioned himself where his grandmother said she'd been that morning. Even after the rain stopped, he could easily tell the cattle and hogs were soaked.

*****

Henry Reinhart's neighbors in Kensington township, and apparently everybody who'd ever heard of him, believed his murder of his brother was only one of a number of misdeeds he'd committed in his quest to own a section of Illinois farmland. Kurt felt he needed to know more.

Arny and Elaine were only too happy to tell him, at length, what they knew, but they couldn't answer many of his most important questions.

Kurt began spending time with several elderly neighbors. Unlike the Boeckers, they'd given up farming themselves and lived off the rent younger neighbors paid to raise crops on their land. Although they had children, they were still as bitter and lonely as the Boeckers. Their sons and daughters and grandchildren, who mostly lived in Kensington or Edinburgh, had other things to do when the old people were too sick or exhausted to put up their storm windows or take them down, to mow their lawns and plant a few flowers in front of their houses, to shovel paths in the snowdrifts to their mailboxes by the road.

Kurt did those things for them. All they had to do was what Edna Boecker had done in the last months of her life—call Elaine and ask for Kurt.

He wouldn't accept their offers to pay him for his work. They possessed something far more valuable than money. They had stories to tell him.

*****

"Otto Reinhart? Your granddad's dad? He had an orchard on top of that hill. Why, in the spring it would look as if he'd gotten a late snow up there all to himself. Everybody in the township could see it. Otto was a good man, even if he didn't go to church."

Otto had left Prussia in his youth to live in a land across the ocean that was said to be free—for European men at least. In America, they not only took votes to determine who among them should govern but also, sometimes like children not getting their way, made the most offensive remarks imaginable when those in power failed to meet their demands.

Otto began speaking as freely as his neighbors did. He was especially supportive of Lincoln's election in 1860. Otto had fled servitude, but the African people in America were slaves. Under the laws of the states permitting slavery, they were considered chattel property with no more rights than a horse or cow had.

Otto's chosen land harbored a strange inconsistency. He wanted it removed. Some of its people—even himself, an immigrant—were as free as they could be. Others weren't free at all.

Kurt had a question for Henry. "How did your father learn to read and write English?"

"He borrowed books from the wealthy people he worked for. They liked him because he was a strong young man and did what he was asked to do without complaining."

*****

In the stories the neighbors told Kurt, the courts in Edinburgh often decided important things. When Elaine and Arny made shopping trips to the city on a weekday when school was out and the clerk's office in the courthouse was open, Kurt would sometimes go along. He'd tell them he wanted to visit the public library and pick up a book or two to read. But once he was out of the car, and the car turned the corner, he'd hurry across the street to the courthouse.

Initially telling the assistant clerks he was working on a school project, he learned how to request the dusty files holding the yellowing documents he wanted to see. He felt the elation of an archeologist during a successful dig whenever he found the papers lawyers had drawn up, judges had signed, clerks had stamped and bailiffs had served giving

His Grandfather's House

Henry what he wanted.

*****

The neighbors told Kurt a mistreated horse had caused the breakage of Lena's stone.

Kurt's grandfather, incensed because the horse, near the end of a hot summer day, had refused to continue working, supposedly gave the animal a whipping.

The poor creature reared up on its hind legs, the neighbors said, and broke away from the hay wagon it was hitched to. It ran from Henry as if for its life and dragged the whippletree up the hill from the barn through the orchard. The crossbar caught Lena's grave marker and "just like that, snapped the horse's neck and cracked the stone."

"Your granddad must've regretted his temper tantrum," one neighbor told Kurt. "People who'd seen the horse thought it was worth a lot of money. Nobody had a tractor then."

"Edna Boecker made that story up," Henry told Kurt. "Your grandmother told her what really happened, but that wasn't good enough for her."

Henry said the horse did break free from the hay wagon. As if crazed, it ran up to and through the orchard. And it fractured Lena's stone and its own neck at the same moment. That was all true. But the horse hadn't refused to work, and Henry hadn't whipped it.

"That mare stepped on a fallen hornets' nest and got herself stung a dozen times at least," Kurt's grandfather said. "I was extremely sorry she killed herself. She was a joy to work with. I admit, though, her death was my fault. The neighbors are right about that. I should've seen the hornets' nest and guided her away from it. It's a farmer's job to protect his animals."

*****

When Henry Reinhart was born in 1888, his half brother, Conrad, was thirty-three, and his half sisters, Lena and Cora, were forty-seven and forty-eight. When Otto Reinhart died in 1911, Henry was twenty-two, Conrad fifty-six, Lena seventy and Cora seventy-one.

At his death, Otto owned 120 acres and the house, barn, orchard and vineyard he'd built and planted. His will, or at least the document filed in probate court purporting to be his will, named Henry the sole heir of his estate. Henry's three half siblings got nothing.

Otto Reinhart supposedly executed his will on January 25, 1911. On that day he was ninety-one years old and had thirty days to live. The signature on his alleged will was a scrawl. The lawyer who drafted the will, Hiram Smith, also owned the Kensington State Bank and later installed his son Chester as its president. Three bank employees signed the will as witnesses.

Conrad and his sisters hired a lawyer to file a petition to contest the will. The pleading alleged, "in the alternative," as the lawyer put it, Otto's signature on the purported will had been forged, Henry had used undue influence on Otto, and Otto was mentally incompetent at the time he allegedly signed his will.

The court never decided those issues.

The judge granted the will-contest petitioners what he said was an "inordinate" number of motions for postponements. Henry told Kurt that was because their lawyer couldn't come up with any evidence to prove their case. The judge set a final date for a hearing on April 5, 1912. But on the third day of March of that year Conrad died.

The lawyer who represented Conrad and his sisters in probate court withdrew from the case. He filed an affidavit stating that Cora and Lena had refused, since Conrad's death, to cooperate with him in the preparation of their case for trial. The court eventually dismissed their will-contest suit for what the dismissal order called "want of prosecution."

Chapter Fifteen

Henry's testimony before a coroner's jury convened in 1912 to consider Conrad's death was consistent with what he told Kurt forty-two years later.

The coroner ruled Conrad's death was accidental. The state's attorney chose not to prosecute Henry. The citizens of Lafayette County, on the other hand, greeted the official version of Conrad's death with intense skepticism.

The sheriff's deputy who'd found Conrad's body publicly agreed with the people. He told a reporter for the *Edinburgh Times* the state's attorney should've prosecuted Henry and let a jury decide whether or not he'd committed murder. The families of the sheriff and the state's attorney, though, were Taft Republican allies. The sheriff fired the deputy, who ran against his former employer in the next election as a Roosevelt Bull Moose Republican—and won.

*****

During a shopping trip with Arny and Elaine to the county seat, twelve-year-old Kurt paid a visit to the *Edinburgh Times* building. He asked to see the articles the newspaper had printed about the 1912 drowning death of his great-uncle, Conrad Reinhart.

The publisher, who'd inherited the paper from his father, invited Kurt to his office and had the articles brought up from the archives department in the basement.

"Those were the first articles I wrote for this paper," the publisher said after Kurt had finished reading them. "I was eighteen. The story went way beyond Lafayette County. All the Chicago papers ran their own articles. It seemed to be a clear case of murder, and yet the guy who did it was going to go free."

"Is it possible," Kurt asked, "it wasn't a murder, and the accused should've gone free?"

"We printed what your grandfather told me," the publisher replied. "I'm sure you saw that. But I don't think he convinced anybody he was telling the truth."

"Didn't the voters pay any attention to what you wrote about the deputy?"

"The business about the deputy having a feud of his own with his family?"

"Yeah. You found out his father had written a will leaving the family farm to his older brother. That's why the younger son became a deputy. His brother had kicked him off the farm. The voters ignored that?"

The publisher sighed. "What I wrote was considered political. My father was a Taft Republican. We didn't endorse the deputy. We backed the sheriff who'd fired him. And we went down to defeat in that election. The voters agreed with the fired deputy. They thought a father should leave his property to all his children."

The publisher looked across his desk at Kurt and shrugged.

"One of your granddad's sisters made an odd remark when I went to see them the day their brother drowned. She said when Henry came back to the house that morning, he was soaked, as if he'd been in the creek himself. But the other sister told her to shut her mouth and keep it shut. The interview was over, she said. The more talkative sister agreed. I'd have to go."

"Maybe my grandfather tried to save his brother's life."

"Or maybe they got into some sort of scuffle down by the creek and both fell in. I didn't print what the sister told me. Neither sister would say anything to the deputies investigating the case. But if they'd been willing to testify about your grandfather being soaked, I'm certain the state's attorney would've had him indicted for murder and forced him to explain it. He'd told the sheriff's people he was nowhere near the creek when his brother fell in. He told me and the coroner's jury the same thing."

*****

On March 23, 1912, less than three weeks after his brother's death, Henry Reinhart married. His bride was the woman who lived on the nearest farm to the west of his. Bertha Hagenbach was thirty years old. Henry was twenty-three.

The old people laughed when they told Kurt about his grandparents' courtship. According to them, Henry went to see Bertha one Saturday night, and on his second visit, the next Saturday evening, he asked her to marry him. Their wedding was the following Saturday.

And since it was "a typical Reinhart wedding," it took place before a justice of the peace.

Bertha was an only child. Her father, Gustav Hagenbach, who was called Gus, owned their 120-acre farm.

But, the neighbors agreed, despite Bertha's advantage of being an only child of a landowning farmer, nobody imagined she'd ever get married.

Five years old when her mother died, she'd grown up in a house only she and her father occupied. Despite her pleas, he refused to let her go to high school, insisting it was a waste of time, especially for a girl.

"That was a big farm for one man," Edna Boecker told Kurt. "Gus needed Bertha to do the work a son would've done."

Bertha, who did the work, became a young woman the neighbors described as "painfully shy" and "reclusive."

"The only time you saw Bertha in public," Edna explained, "it was Christmas or Easter, and she was in the back row at Cecil's church, alone. Her father, like your grandfather, didn't attend church. Gus did the shopping for both of them. You never saw Bertha in a store. She ordered her clothes and personal things out of a Sears catalogue."

When Bertha informed her father of her intention to marry their neighbor, he let her know, Edna said, his opposition to her marriage to a man who'd murdered his brother was total.

Bertha, though, apparently neglected to make Henry aware, during their one-week engagement, of her father's objections. Otherwise, Edna and the other neighbors agreed, Henry surely would've backed out of that wedding.

The evening of the day Bertha married Henry, her father showed up drunk at the wedding celebration, such as it was, in the Reinhart house on the hill. The only others in attendance were the bridal couple, the groom's two elderly half sisters and Edna and Karl Boecker.

Bertha's father loudly accused his new son-in-law of murder.

"You pushed your own brother into that creek," he yelled at Henry. "I know you did it, you devil. You killed him to get your father's farm."

Henry's half sisters became hysterical, holding one another and weeping.

Henry opened his back door and ordered his new bride's father to leave his house.

The older man refused and instead renewed his drunken allegations.

Henry grabbed him by his coat collar, marched him across the kitchen and gave him a shove through the doorway that landed him facedown in the day's early-spring snow.

Through a kitchen window, the bride watched her father stagger to his feet.

Many neighbors wondered why Bertha married Henry in the face of her father's accusations. Edna, though, said Bertha had scoffed at them from the beginning.

"Henry was her prince," Edna said. "He'd rescued her from a lifetime of spinsterhood."

Edna Boecker wasn't the only neighbor who let Kurt know his grandfather's youthful good looks, which nobody disputed, might've had something to do with the matter as well.

Edna also told Kurt that when Bertha peered through the kitchen window of her new home on her wedding night and saw her drunken father covered with mud and snow, she openly laughed.

*****

Bertha knew her father, Henry's recently deceased older brother, Conrad, and another bachelor neighbor had been drinking companions. She was aware that nights when her father left her in their house by herself his destination wasn't a tavern in Kensington or Edinburgh. It was Albert Rauenthaler's house.

There, Gus Hagenbach drank the beer his host made, as well as the wine and hard cider Conrad got from his father every Saturday after the Reinharts' work for the week was done.

When Bertha and Henry married, Gus still owned his 120 acres free and clear. During the previous decade, though, he'd been selling off his livestock and machinery to pay his bills. In the autumn of 1910 he sold his last horse.

The neighbors assumed the reason for his heavy drinking was to drown his sorrow over losing his wife. Although Bertha knew that wasn't so, she couldn't come up with any other excuse for it—not to Edna's satisfaction at least.

During the last few years before Conrad died, Gus had increasingly borrowed Otto Reinhart's equipment and horses to work his fields. Conrad, the story went, interceded with his father, year after year, on behalf of their neighbor. According to Conrad, Gus was simply down on his luck.

But Henry openly criticized his father for giving in, most of all whenever it meant their own field work might be delayed.

Otto tried to silence his younger son by telling him it would be impossible for the three of them—Otto, Conrad and Henry—to get behind in the work needed to be done on their 120 acres. Otto was right, but he neglected to acknowledge his contention was well-founded only because Henry did most of the work.

During the growing season in 1911, though, after Otto's death, Henry made no objection when Conrad used the Reinharts' machinery and horses to help Gus and his daughter plant and bring in their crops.

When Bertha worked with her father and Conrad, the neighbors agreed, she was like Henry when he worked with his father and Conrad. She accomplished more than the other two combined.

In late May of the next year, after Conrad had died and Bertha had married, Henry could see Gus was making no effort to begin his field work. Henry asked Bertha to go to her father with their offer to help him.

Gus refused to allow Bertha inside his house. As for her new husband, Gus wouldn't permit "that murdering Cain" to come onto his property for any reason.

Gus planted no crops in 1912, let his fields grow up to weeds and reaped no harvest.

One Saturday evening in October of that year, Gus failed to show up at Albert Rauenthaler's for their usual drinking session.

The next morning, Albert found him hanging by a rope from a beam in the hayloft in the Hagenbach barn.

Gus had left a self-described "SUICIDE NOTE" on his kitchen table. In it, he blamed his "untimely death" on his daughter, who'd abandoned him "to fornicate with a man who murdered his own brother!"

"That's when Albert let everybody know he'd seen the light," Edna told Kurt.

"What light had he seen?" Kurt asked.

"He'd lost both of his drinking companions in the same year. He'd therefore decided to throw away his beer and swear off alcohol and all his other sins forever."

Chapter Sixteen

Soon after Gus Hagenbach's funeral, which Henry didn't attend, Bertha received a letter from a lawyer. Her father had made out a will in which he'd named as his sole heir and legatee a nephew who lived in Chicago and had never seen the farm.

For her many years of hard work, Bertha got nothing.

Bertha's cousin, Claude Hagenbach, was thirty-five. He'd worked in a factory since quitting high school at sixteen. He and his wife had four young children and no savings.

And, like his uncle, Edna told Kurt, he was partial to drinking.

During the winter after Gus hanged himself, and before Claude and his family were able to move out to the farm from Chicago, the Hagenbach barn burned to the ground.

"There was no reason in this world," the old people told Kurt, "why that empty barn should've caught fire. Excepting a neighbor wanted the Hagenbach land for himself. The barn wasn't filled with green hay getting hot. There was no lightning storm that night. Not in the middle of February."

Once again, on the other hand, the authorities couldn't come up with any proof Henry had committed a crime.

He stated his theory as to the origin of the fire to the reporter from the *Edinburgh Times*, the publisher's son. A drunken tramp from the road had gone into the barn and set a fire to keep warm. The fire had gotten out of hand, and the tramp had fled.

Henry thereafter rebuked, with a cold and silent stare, the few people, including Kurt, who dared to question his view of the matter.

In any event, no insurance covered the loss. Several years previously, without letting Bertha know, Gus had stopped paying for it. And Claude hadn't thought to buy any.

*****

Claude Hagenbach had to pay off his uncle's debts and the costs, including attorney fees, of probating his estate. He also needed money to replace the horses and equipment his uncle had sold off, and to pay the expenses his family would incur before he brought in his first harvest.

But Claude hadn't established any credit in Lafayette County—or anywhere else for that matter. He could find no bank willing to lend money to a farmer who had no farming experience.

What happened next surprised the neighbors. Henry and Bertha were willing to lend him whatever he and his family needed to get by. Claude had to sign some legal documents giving them a mortgage on his farm, but they required no repayments from him for two years. By then, Claude told the neighbors, he'd have the proceeds from two harvests, which would no doubt be more than enough to pay off his debt to them, and the interest on it, in full.

Henry and Bertha were in a position to make such a loan. Otto had left Henry not only 120 acres of farmland, a house, an outsize barn and livestock but also accounts at the Kensington State Bank. And the years prior to the First World War were favorable for farmers in Lafayette County. Henry, having inherited his father's strong back and willingness to work, as the neighbors put it, gained as much from the prosperity as any farmer in the county.

But for Claude the good times meant nothing. At the end of 1913, his first year on the farm, he was still borrowing money from Bertha and Henry just to put food on the table and keep his family alive.

Nevertheless, Claude was confident his second year would be different. He admitted to Bertha he'd started out assuming he didn't need to know anything about farming.

"I thought," he told her, "anybody could do it."

Claude, though, faced two substantial problems.

First, the hard work required of him in the fields in the spring, summer and fall, to which he wasn't accustomed or suited, drove him to seek the solace of the tavern in Kensington. Because its proprietors wouldn't extend credit to him, he had to buy his liquor with the money he should've used to pay his family's bills for groceries, hardware, farm implements and drugstore items—the bills Bertha and Henry paid and added to the balance of Claude's promissory note.

Claude's second problem was having no barn to store his crops. He therefore had to sell them, skimpy as they were, to Hiram Smith, who owned the grain elevator next to the railroad tracks in Kensington—and at the depressed prices they brought during harvest time.

Late in the winter of 1915, after spending more than two futile years on his uncle's farm and facing another season of tedious field work, Claude decided to sell his farm. The only persons willing to make a bid on it, though, were Henry and Bertha. Every other prospective buyer could see Claude owed more on his debt to them than his farm was worth.

Claude therefore took no money with him when his sale to Bertha and Henry closed. All he got was the buyers' forgiveness of the debt he owed them.

For a year or so after Claude and his family returned to Chicago penniless, he sent letters to Bertha pleading for another loan.

Bertha replied to each of his requests with a polite refusal, and always for the same reason. She and Henry had decided Claude and his family would be better off if they learned to fend for themselves.

In her last letter, Bertha included a paragraph Henry not only approved but praised for being so nicely worded.

"We've heard," Bertha wrote, "the factories in Chicago are busy these days supplying the armies fighting in Europe. We're certain the owners and managers of those plants can use all the good, steady workers they can find."

*****

Arnold Otto Reinhart was born on January 15, 1913.

Bertha was glad Arny couldn't remember living the first two years of his life in the house on the hill with his mother, father and Henry's elderly half sisters.

"Those two drank wine in their room upstairs," Bertha told Kurt. "They usually came down to supper drunk. They'd start talking about their deceased brother. They'd get louder and louder. They'd end up accusing Henry of murdering Conrad."

Henry would continue eating his meal and let them wear themselves out. Then he'd close the argument with a remark such as the one Bertha remembered word for word.

"If you really think I murdered your brother," he'd told his half sisters, "you should thank me for it. I'm keeping you alive. Conrad would've let you die."

After Cousin Claude and his family moved out of the Hagenbach house down by the road, Henry decided he'd had enough of his sisters.

He, Bertha and Arny would live in the Hagenbach house. And the sisters would remain behind in the house on the hill.

Henry paid to put plumbing and electricity in the Hagenbach house. Bertha told the neighbors she'd found herself in heaven in her own house.

The half sisters, though, never enjoyed indoor plumbing and electricity. According to the neighbors, Henry's failure to provide them with the same amenities he enjoyed was one more offense he'd committed on a list of many.

Nobody, on the other hand, had anything good to say about Cora and Lena.

"They were two of the meanest, nastiest people who ever lived," Edna Boecker told Kurt. "Whenever they went to town, which wasn't often, thank God, the younger children thought they were witches. They always wore black. In memory of their brother, they said. They told anybody who'd listen to them Conrad's ghost often visited the house they lived in. He begged them, they said, to take revenge on the man who'd killed him."

At that point in her story, Edna tittered.

"The sisters would even tell young children that story," she said. "You should've seen those kids as soon they saw your great-aunts coming down Main Street toward them. They'd run to their parents, some of them screaming."

Edna's remarks about the children hadn't surprised Kurt. One young boy Cora and Lena had told their story to was Arny.

*****

When Henry moved back into the house on the hill after Bertha died, he told Kurt he could sleep and store his clothes and other possessions wherever he wished on the second floor. That gave Kurt a choice of three rooms. Which one he slept in depended upon the season.

In the winter, he chose the room looking south. Through its windows he could see houses and barns clumped together on the snow-covered prairie like clusters of microbes in a Petri dish. That was Lena and Cora's room from their childhood to their deaths in the winter of 1921-1922.

In the spring, Kurt slept in the room on the east side of the house.

His Grandfather's House

Through its windows he could watch the sun and moon rise over Otto's orchard. A time always came in May when blossoms covered the few remaining apple trees like swarms of pink-and-white moths. This was the room Otto and his two wives had slept in. It was also Henry and Bertha's bedroom during the first years of their marriage.

In the summer and autumn, Kurt claimed the room facing west and north.

Conrad was in his thirties when his infant brother, Henry, had joined him in this room. They shared a bed until their father died.

Then a bailiff brought the court papers informing Henry's half siblings that Otto had executed a will leaving everything to Henry. The bailiff read the documents for them.

Conrad told Henry he'd rather see him dead than the sole owner of their father's farm.

Henry responded to his brother's threat by moving his clothes and other belongings into his father's room. After that, he slept in Otto's room—and, until Conrad died in the flooding creek, with the door locked.

The room facing west and north was also the room where Arny had found Johnny dead.

Chapter Seventeen

After Conrad Reinhart and Gus Hagenbach died in 1912, their drinking companion, Albert Rauenthaler, admitted they'd never invited women to their get-togethers at his house. Nor did women, after the death of Gus's wife twenty-five years earlier, appear to have played much of a part in the social lives of the three men. Albert, an only child who'd inherited his farm when he was still in his early twenties, said he and his two friends also hadn't invited any other men to drink with them.

The neighbors had wondered about the three men but ultimately decided they weren't guilty of anything more serious than drinking too much. People who engaged in the more odious activity in question, they agreed, didn't live on farms or in small towns.

When Kurt chose to discuss the subject one evening at the dining room table, his grandfather's response surprised him.

"You're free to believe whatever those neighbors tell you," Henry said. "Just remember, the reality of the matter might be something else."

Kurt believed he knew what the something else was.

The Lafayette County Library in Edinburgh included a section of books for lawyers. But Kurt had discovered he didn't have to be a lawyer or even an adult to read them.

He found in section 141 of the Illinois Criminal Code the reason no one would confess to doing what the neighbors agreed Albert, Gus and Conrad hadn't done. It had long been the law in Illinois. A court could send a person who'd committed the "infamous crime against nature, either with man or beast," to prison for up to ten years.

*****

Edna Boecker told Kurt a story about Arny he hadn't heard before.

When Arny's school year came to an end in the spring of 1922, he was nine years old. The aunts he'd been afraid of were dead. He could venture out of the house by himself.

Henry took him down to the barn and out to the fields to work.

Arny cried, though, in the summer when it was hot and in the winter when it was cold.

After well more than a year of trying to get what Henry called some decent work out of the boy, he was ready to give up.

"He's not much use to me at all," he complained to Bertha.

He asked her if she'd consider having another child.

"She was in her forties by then," Edna told Kurt, "but it was the happiest day of her life."

She gave birth to Johnny on October 23, 1924.

*****

After Henry bought the Hagenbach farm in 1915, he worked every day of the week.

"Every day," Bertha told Kurt, "sunrise to sunset, rain or shine, Sundays and holidays included. He had two hundred forty acres to work and livestock to feed and tend."

He did much of his work with his five horses. He'd inherited his father's stallion and mare. He soon bought three additional, unrelated mares. One of the mares was always bearing or suckling a foal. That horse and her foal stayed in the barn in the winter and roamed the creek land and woods in the spring, summer and fall. The stallion and the other three mares worked in teams of two, under the harness one day, resting in the barn or woods the next. Henry would yearly sell a foal that cost him little more than the feed it had eaten.

When efficient gasoline-powered tractors became available in the mid-1920s, Henry Reinhart was the first person in Kensington township to make a purchase. He paid for the machine with cash from his considerable savings, which he'd recently increased with the proceeds from the sale of his horses.

The farm implement dealer in Edinburgh who sold the tractor to Henry laughed when he heard Reverend Crosley had informed his congregants a money changer had accepted Satan's lucre for a newfangled machine.

"I can't believe Reinhart's checks come from Satan," the dealer said. "Henry's never given me a check my bank and his won't accept. And if they take his checks, why can't I?"

*****

"Your grandfather," a neighbor told Kurt, "chose to use his land to raise cattle and hogs for the stockyards in Chicago. He did it well. He put his profits in the bank. He also let his father Otto's orchard become a weedy, tangled thicket. And it used to be so beautiful in the spring."

"That damned orchard," Henry told Kurt, "never brought my father enough money to justify the time and effort he put into it."

He looked at his grandson across Otto's dining room table.

"And don't forget," he said, "what came from his apple trees and grape vines."

"What was that?"

"Hard cider and wine," Henry explained. "The booze my brother and sisters got drunk on every damned day of their lives."

Henry had no rule regarding the use of alcohol in his houses. Bertha, Arny and Elaine had always been free to drink it. Like him, though, they'd chosen not to.

On the other hand, even Prohibition hadn't stopped his half sisters from drinking. Their only purpose in going to town—and frightening the children—was to buy, with the money Henry gave them, the sweet wine they freely admitted they couldn't live without.

The seller was a woman almost as old as they were. She lived off the proceeds from the sale of the wine she made from the Concord grapes she grew on her five acres just outside Kensington. Early on, the people from Chicago who ran the alcohol business in Lafayette County during Prohibition made an exception for her. She didn't have to pay for their protection.

*****

The late 1920s, the neighbors agreed, were bad years for farmers, just as bad as the 1930s would be for everybody. The nation's Great Depression, Kurt read in a book he'd found in the county library, began on its farms.

But while the low prices for farm commodities reduced Henry's annual profits, he never suffered a loss, Depression year or not. He even showed his skeptical grandson his financial records, carefully handwritten in pencil, to prove it.

Like the Boeckers, the owners of the other eighty-acre farms in the section kept dairy cattle and lived on their monthly milk checks. But their land didn't produce enough to feed their herds. That forced them to buy corn and hay from those who had it to sell.

"Like your granddad," Edna told Kurt.

Henry could store his bountiful crops of grain in the large corncrib he'd paid carpenters to build during the First World War. He had ample room in the upper story of his father's barn, with its hand-hewn beams, for his hay and straw.

Corn, oats and hay were inexpensive in late summer, fall and early winter when they were plentiful. But their price underwent a transmutation, like a chrysalis becoming a butterfly, in late winter when they became scarce. The eighty-acre dairy farmers had to buy feed for their cows with money they should've used to pay down their debts.

*****

Ruth and Walter Riegel owned the eighty-acre farm legally described as "the east half of the northwest quarter" of the section. It lay between the Boeckers' eighty-acre farm and Albert's.

The Riegels' older son died in a trench in the First World War. The Germans killed him with mustard gas.

Henry Reinhart was almost twenty-nine years old when Woodrow Wilson took the United States into the war in April 1917. Henry had a family of five to feed and a farm of 240 acres to work. Whether it was his good luck or not, he never received a notice from the draft board.

"And I didn't see any reason to volunteer to fight," he later told Kurt. "Not in a damned foolish war only the idiot emperors, monarchs and prime ministers of Europe could dream up. My father came to this country to get away from that."

In the early 1920s, the younger Riegel son quit high school when he was a junior. Within a week, his reason for doing so became clear. He left for the west coast with a young barber he'd met in Edinburgh.

Every few months after that, he'd send his mother a tearful, homesick-sounding letter. But he wouldn't reveal where he was, and his envelopes bore no return address. He was afraid, he explained, his parents would contact the authorities and make him come home—home to the farm he'd seemed to love as a child but now professed to hate. He promised his mother he'd let her know his whereabouts after he turned twenty-one.

He and his friend were in love, he wrote, and "will gladly go to hell for it if we have to."

The Riegels' daughter, their middle child, met a man from Chicago in a new speakeasy in an old barn a mile down a lane off the road between Kensington and Edinburgh. He drove an expensive car and gave her clothes and jewelry that she, a teacher in the Kensington elementary school who walked with a slight limp from a case of polio in her teens, couldn't afford.

He was at least twenty years older than she was, but she married him before a justice of the peace anyway and moved to Chicago. Less than a month after the wedding, the sheriff's deputies found her husband dead in the trunk of his car in the dirt parking lot behind the speakeasy. He'd told the owners of the place he was collecting protection money for Capone's people. He was in fact keeping it for himself.

Some people said Capone had paid the Riegels' daughter to spy on her husband and bring him down. Her next marriage was to a man the neighbors claimed was a legitimate member of the mob.

"She was lucky, too," they told Kurt. "He was a damned good-looking dago."

With all their children gone, the Riegels took a hired man into their house.

"After they'd lost their older boy in the war and their other two children ran off," an elderly neighbor told Kurt, "Walt no longer had it in him to do much farming. Ruth got to where she'd burst into tears if anybody mentioned their children."

Within a few months on the job, the Riegels' hired man—nobody seemed to know where he came from—had antagonized the entire Kensington community. He never bothered to attend Cecil's church, but if he had, he would've heard himself assailed from the pulpit as Satan's serpent.

He'd begun spending his employers' money as if it were his own. At the poker table in the back room of the speakeasy, he taunted his opponents with the suggestion that if the money he was gambling with wasn't his, how could he lose?

The question was additionally provocative because it seldom needed to be answered. When the hired man played cards, he almost always won.

"Then one day he left the Riegels and Kensington without saying good-by," the neighbors told Kurt. "And he took a lot of their money with him. He'd withdrawn his stash bit by bit from their account at the Kensington State Bank."

Many years later, the mere memory of the man's audacity was enough to bring Edna Boecker to tears. Why had the Riegels been so foolish as to allow their hired man access to their bank account? Both Walter and Ruth had finished high school. They were people who read books and kept up on current events in magazines and newspapers. They clearly should've known better.

The neighbors were divided on the issue. Some believed the Riegels' misfortunes concerning their children had driven them both insane, easy prey for the first predator who came along.

Others hinted Ruth might've been too fond of the hired man, who wasn't much older than her first son would've been. He was more attentive to her, she confided to Edna after he'd absconded, than she'd believed a man could be.

In 1928, the chancery court in Edinburgh entered an order of foreclosure on the Riegels' eighty acres.

Henry Reinhart was the successful bidder at the sale.

He and Bertha then owned 320 acres of the section, and he was halfway to his goal.

Chapter Eighteen

Anna and Wilbur Linden owned "the east half of the northeast quarter," the eighty-acre farm next to Albert Rauenthaler's "west half of the northeast quarter."

When she was in her forties, Anna gave birth to Marie, her and Wilbur's only child.

Previously, Anna and Wilbur had equally shared both the outdoor and indoor work on their farm. But after Anna became pregnant, Wilbur had to perform most of the outdoor work by himself, and without Anna at his side to tell him what to do next.

When she was eighteen, Marie married Dieter, the younger of two sons of tenant farmers. The neighbors called them "an exceptionally attractive couple." Within three years, Marie and Dieter had three children.

"Marie explained it for me," Edna told Kurt. "She, unlike her barnyard-loving mother, didn't intend to wait around to have children until she was too old to do it properly."

Although the income from the eighty-acre farm couldn't support a family consisting of four adults and three children, Marie and Dieter felt they could only stay and make the best of it. Even if that meant they had to help Anna and Wilbur do the work that kept them and their children alive. Anna had made it clear to Marie and Dieter they'd inherit nothing if they left the farm and forced Anna and Wilbur to take in a hired man.

Dieter soon called himself Anna and Wilbur's "slave." He thought he was fit, smart and aggressive enough to do the outdoor work, but he could only do it the way Anna and Wilbur told him to. And they often seemed confused.

One year they waited far too long to give him their order to begin the spring planting. He was still working on it in June, he told Edna Boecker, when he should've been taking in their first crop of hay. The yields for all their crops were meager, laughable in comparison with Henry Reinhart's, even on a per-acre basis.

At the poker table, Dieter complained under his breath that if he'd known what he was getting himself into, he never would've married Anna and Wilbur Linden's daughter.

The Riegels' hired man looked up from his cards and gave Dieter a knowing grin.

"Just remember," he said, "those old people aren't going to live forever."

"The sooner they die the better," Dieter agreed. "I'll be free of them."

"That's more like it," the hired man said.

He ordered and paid for another drink for Dieter.

But Dieter's luck at the speakeasy card table in the evening was no better than it was on the Linden farm during the day. Dieter considered himself worse off than the Riegels' hired man, who was free to do the farmwork and spend his employers' money as he pleased. How did that get turned around? Didn't sons-in-law rank higher than hired men?

Dieter found another form of consolation from the disappointment his efforts on the Linden farm had brought him. In his last year in high school, which he'd chosen to end early to marry Marie, she wasn't the one he'd most wanted. He'd had his eye on the Kensington mailman's daughter, who'd somehow failed to notice his physical appeal and desire for her and married the second son of the Kensington grocers instead.

She began to see what an attractive man Dieter was only after her own husband left her and their four children one day as abruptly as death from a gunshot wound to the head.

What could the husband's family do but go on providing the mailman's daughter and their four young grandchildren with the necessities of life? And act as if they didn't know how often, after poker at the speakeasy, Dieter parked his car in the alley behind the tiny house where their daughter-in-law and her children lived?

But their neighbors knew, and they spoke of it to others.

In the late 1920s, Anna and Wilbur Linden died within months of each other. They left their farm to Marie but only as the trustee for their three grandchildren. Under the terms of the trust, when the last child turned twenty-one, the three of them would inherit the farm.

Their will made no mention of Dieter.

Several years before they died, Anna and Wilbur had obtained a mortgage loan from the Kensington State Bank and used the proceeds to pay their family's day-to-day expenses. In each of the following years, the debt grew. After they died, the bank told Marie she'd have to begin making payments on the loan. Dieter wondered why he should put in the long hours of hard work needed to do that. He'd never own the farm no matter what he did. He'd continue, he said, as a "slave," now to his and Marie's three children instead of Marie's parents.

"And the first thing they'll do," he told the Riegels' hired man, "they'll throw their philandering father out on his ass. If I was in their shoes, that's what I'd do."

Following that logic, Dieter spent time in the speakeasy and backseat of his car he could've used to save his children's farm, and, despite his forgivable errors, earn their gratitude.

Marie lost the farm in a chancery court proceeding in 1931.

At the foreclosure sale—which drew the righteous indignation of a crowd of onlookers, some of them loudly giving voice to it—a bidding war began for Marie's eighty acres.

Henry Reinhart's surprise adversary was a speculator in Edinburgh on other business who apparently thought he might pick up a parcel of northern Illinois farmland for a song.

The crowd cheered for a man they referred to among themselves as a "Chicago Jew." Whether they were right about that or not, he didn't make the winning bid.

When the auctioneer lowered his gavel to conclude the sale, Henry and Bertha owned 400 acres of the section.

*****

Alberta and Frederick Warner owned the eighty acres to the east of Otto Reinhart's farm, "the east half of the southeast quarter." Like the Lindens, they had one child. The name on his birth certificate was Victor, but he was called Vic.

The neighbors told Kurt both Alberta and Frederick had the kind of hefty, big-boned bodies they needed to perform the work a dairy farm required.

Vic grew up hearing the same words used to describe him. In the 1920s, he played on the Kensington High School football team and became what the sports editor for the *Edinburgh Times* called "the most powerful athlete Lafayette County has ever seen."

As a lineman on defense, he often plowed through the offensive line as if it hadn't taken the field. All too soon he had his arms wrapped around whichever opposing back had the ball.

As the fullback on offense, he was slow and methodical, but he was also unstoppable once he gained enough momentum. The only defenders able to outrun him were slighter and smaller than he was. Vic brushed those opponents aside, the sports editor wrote, "as if they were flies on a horse's tail."

The teams Vic played for during his junior and senior years never lost a game. And those were the only unbeaten teams in the history of Kensington High.

When his last season came to an end, though, Vic faced an uncertain future. He couldn't imagine going to college in order to continue playing football. He was afraid people would see him as he saw himself, "stupid." He detested sitting in a classroom. He hated reading books.

He made his mother and father send away the college coaches and their assistants who came to recruit him to play for their teams.

He couldn't deny, though, the football field and the uproar that came with it, especially the cries of joy from the stands, had made sense to him. Working on his parents' farm didn't.

Without football, only his mother's meals satisfied him. As she'd done during his playing years, she heaped on his plate all the meat and potatoes and pie and ice cream he could handle.

"Vic," Alberta explained to Edna, "is my only child."

In Vic's senior year in high school, the cheerleader his teammates most wanted to share a backseat with had been his girlfriend. The Kensington community assumed Vic would marry Gwendolyn, and she'd live with him on the Warners' farm.

Their dating, though, wasn't what Vic's teammates had imagined it to be. Vic and Gwendolyn would meet at the Kensington Christian Church, and she'd go home with him and his parents for Alberta's Sunday dinners, which Vic claimed couldn't be duplicated this side of heaven. After the feast, he'd drive Gwendolyn home.

But when Vic stopped playing football, he began putting on weight. Gwendolyn soon made excuses for not joining his family for their Sunday dinner after church.

One day, word came down from Kensington that Gwendolyn was enjoying the company of Chester Smith. His father, Hiram Smith, had promised him he'd become president of the Kensington State Bank as soon as he graduated from college.

Vic claimed not to care if Gwendolyn preferred a potential

banker to a mere son of farmers. He realized his football glory was meaningless. Alberta's food, though, never disappointed. It became as vital to him as football had been.

"All three of those Warners," Edna told Kurt, "took to eating as if nothing else in life mattered."

As the years passed, their bodies grew larger and weaker. They suffered severe shortness of breath while cleaning house, shoveling manure or carrying feed to the cows. During the planting season one year, they all three complained of chest pain.

But they agreed not to hire anybody to help them.

"How do you suppose that would've looked?" Edna asked Kurt. "With a grown son, a former football player, in the kitchen helping his mother bake cookies, cakes and pies?"

Vic suggested they retire as dairy farmers. He proposed they sell their cow herd, two horses and machinery and rent their land to a neighboring farmer. Vic assumed the three of them could live comfortably as landlords.

They soon learned, though, the money their neighbors were willing to pay to work their land at that point in the 1930s wouldn't cover their grocery, coal and tax bills. Any repayment of the money they'd borrowed from the Kensington State Bank whenever their milk checks hadn't been sufficient to cover their needs was out of the question.

They also learned any new loan money from the bank was equally hopeless.

Henry Reinhart was the only bidder at the sheriff's sale of their farm.

*****

Nobody told the Riegels, Lindens and Warners the money they'd borrowed at the Kensington State Bank wasn't the bank's money. It was Henry's.

"If they'd known where the money was coming from," Edna told Kurt, "they might've mended their ways."

In the courthouse in Edinburgh, Kurt discovered how his grandfather had concealed his loans to his improvident neighbors. He'd done it through trust agreements he'd made with the bank. The dairy farmers either never noticed or understood why the promissory notes and mortgage deeds they were so grateful to sign ran in favor of the bank as trustee. The bank was the trustee, but Henry was the beneficiary of the trust and therefore the real "party of the first part" who loaned the money and held the mortgage in the notes and deeds.

Whenever the debts of his neighbors rose to the point where they were equal to what he wished to pay for their land, he would instruct the bank not to lend them another penny. Because they'd already defaulted on their debts to him, he was also entitled to direct the bank, as his trustee, to file foreclosure petitions against them in chancery court.

When the court ordered the sale of their farms, Henry was certain to make the highest bids. He was merely paying himself what they owed him.

On their moving days, the departing Riegels, Lindens and Warners cursed and shook their fists as their neighbor in his Model T Ford drove past them in the other direction.

Staring straight ahead, ignoring them, Henry was on his way to take possession of what they'd mistakenly believed would be their homes forever.

They might've mended their ways if they'd known the truth? Kurt came down on his grandfather's side of that question. Possibly— therefore the secret trusts—but not likely.

Edna Boecker herself took Henry's money and expressed no regret for doing it.

Chapter Nineteen

Kurt wondered if his grandfather didn't appreciate his older son enough. Arny stayed on the farm where he'd been born, apparently never dreamed of another kind of life, and did whatever his father told him to do no matter how much he disliked doing it.

Arny married Elaine in October of 1939, soon after another war in Europe had begun. Elaine was thirty-five. Arny was twenty-six.

Elaine's father and mother were tenant farmers in Lafayette County who both died young. Tuberculosis claimed her mother when Elaine, their only child, was in her senior year in high school. A heart attack took her father when she was twenty-five.

Elaine, who'd been doing all the indoor work and most of the outdoor labor even before her father died, wanted to remain on the farm. But the landlady, a widow without children, told her renting farmland to a single woman was unheard of and ridiculous.

Elaine obtained a job in the Sears store in Edinburgh. She moved into a one-bedroom apartment above a drugstore a block away. Her efficiency and candor in selling men's and boys' clothing impressed Bertha, who bought all her husband's and sons' clothes at Sears.

Even when he was quite young, Arny had enjoyed going with his mother on her shopping trips. And Henry was glad he did. Somebody had to go with Bertha whenever she went to town. Arny's penchant for it relieved Henry of the need to perform that task.

Arny found Elaine amusing.

The day after their Friday evening wedding, before the same justice of the peace who would later marry Kurt's mother and father, Elaine helped Henry, Arny and fifteen-year-old Johnny pick corn.

Both Henry and Bertha, who then owned 480 acres, thanked her at the supper table.

Elaine continued doing outdoor work.

"She was like Anna Linden," Edna told Kurt. "She enjoyed it. She didn't mind the heat and the cold and the dust."

Bertha, though, was in her late fifties. She confessed to Elaine in tears one day she was getting too old to keep a proper home for five people.

She also told Elaine she often felt lonely in the house by herself.

"And the one person in this family I'd most like to be in this house with is you," Bertha said. "I love my husband and my sons. Don't get me wrong. But what more can I say?"

Elaine had recently happened upon Johnny masturbating in the barn. The second time she did, he refused to stop even after she'd faked a cough to make her presence known to him. Stopping was a courtesy he invariably extended to his father and brother without their needing to ask for it.

Elaine began working inside the house and gave up all her outside work except feeding the chickens, gathering their eggs, and butchering them when their time came.

*****

Henry didn't oppose the new arrangement. Although he often acted as if housework was beneath his notice, he realized somebody had to do it—somebody other than himself.

He could also see Bertha was "slowing down," as the neighbors put it, and would soon be unable to do her work. Besides, he felt he could count on Johnny to do a good portion of the outside work Elaine had been doing.

Within a matter of a few weeks inside the house, Elaine had reduced her mother-in-law to the status of a helpmate.

Bertha didn't complain. Nor did anybody else in the Reinhart household.

Henry went so far as to warn Johnny never to go near the chicken coop.

*****

Every Saturday afternoon Henry paid Arny, Elaine and Johnny what they all referred to as "wages" for the work they'd done that week. The payees were free to spend the money however they pleased.

Bertha also had full access to all of Henry's bank accounts. When Arny grew old enough to buy personal items for himself, Henry told Bertha to give him whatever she thought he needed to pay for them. Her reimbursements were in addition to Arny's wages.

Henry's rule later applied to Johnny and Elaine as well. And Bertha was generous.

Extravagant purchases, though—for items such as an electric stove or a television—required Henry's approval.

His Grandfather's House

*****

Arny was twenty-eight years old when the Japanese attack on Pearl Harbor brought the Second World War to America. Having no children, he feared being drafted.

Johnny was seventeen. Defying his father and using the excuse that he'd soon be dead anyway, he quit high school and began drinking.

He stayed out late on weekends with the young people from Kensington and neighboring towns who congregated in the taverns in Lafayette County serving alcohol to underage drinkers. He could easily walk to and from the most popular one. It was in the barn at the end of the lane off the blacktop road between Kensington and Edinburgh—the Capone speakeasy during Prohibition. It was now known as Al's Place.

Despite Johnny's drinking, Henry never stopped paying him his wages for his work. Johnny somehow still got to the barn every morning in time to feed the livestock with his father and brother.

He didn't deny his mother's charge at the breakfast table one morning he smelled of alcohol and cigarette smoke.

He returned his father's glare with one of his own. "I don't smoke. But I also don't tell other people how to live their lives. Most of my friends choose to smoke. Is it surprising I smell the way they do?"

Henry shrugged his shoulders and bought the story. None of the Reinharts had seen Johnny smoking on the farm.

*****

The owners and male patrons of Al's Place favored Lorelei Juergen. They saw to it she never had to pay for a drink. She didn't drink that much in any event.

Late in the summer of 1942, she chose Johnny Reinhart to be her boyfriend. She soon let him do what he wanted with her, but only if he wore a rubber. Her friends agreed he was more than good-looking enough to, as they put it, "go all the way with." Besides, his father owned a lot of land, and people said they could only dream of having as much money in the bank as they'd heard he had.

Johnny thought Lorelei's choosing him to be her boyfriend was the miracle he'd been waiting for. He began drinking less, too.

115

Henry let Johnny use his car to take Lorelei to the movies in Edinburgh.

"That's not all he used Henry's car for," Elaine told Kurt. "We heard about it from everybody between her house and Edinburgh. One of those nights in that car they must've started you on your way into this world. Those rubbers sometimes break. Or they don't get put on as promised."

*****

After Lorelei married Johnny on Christmas Eve in 1942, the Reverend Cecil Crosley chose to include in his sermons warnings of eternal damnation for any young woman "willing to trade her nubile body for Lucifer's filthy lucre."

Cecil provided a lengthy description, using words not often heard from a pulpit, of the physical desirability of one such person he'd recently observed "strutting down Main Street in this very town, shamelessly displaying the evidence of her premarital sin."

Talk like that about the Reinhart family, who never required naming, packed Cecil's House of God.

"The schoolteachers who go to that Episcopalian church in Edinburgh," Cecil told Edna Boecker, "can laugh at me all they want. I'm telling the people what God wants me to tell them. My sermons are about sin and those among us who choose to sin."

*****

The neighbors agreed that in one matter at least, Henry Reinhart had been law-abiding to a fault. During the Second World War, unlike many of his neighbors, he refused to sell any of his livestock to the black market buyers, many of them the same people who'd run the speakeasies during Prohibition.

Some people thought Henry knew as well as anybody else the authorities in charge of rationing would look the other way if they heard some small farmer had sold a few cattle or hogs on the black market.

"But Henry, with his big farm," one typical neighbor said, "they would've nailed him. He was too scared he'd get caught. He refused to sell even after the black market people threatened to rustle his cattle and hogs off his property in the middle of the night. He let them know they'd deeply regret trying to do that. He had a shotgun, he told them, and he knew how to use it."

Kurt's grandfather disagreed with that story only in regard to his motivation.

"Rationing was a stupid law, like Prohibition," he told Kurt, "but it was the law. To get what I've wanted in this world, I've never needed to break a law. Despite what our bigmouth neighbors tell you, it's as simple as that."

Chapter Twenty

In the autumn of 1956, Albert Rauenthaler, then eighty years old, felt unwell. After spending a week in bed, he reluctantly drove himself to Edinburgh to see the doctor Arny had called when Bertha suffered the illness that led to her death.

The doctor gave Albert a shot, prescribed some pills and sent him home.

*****

The next day, thirteen-year-old Kurt, who'd begun eighth grade in September, walked to Albert's house after school and knocked on his door.

"Who is it?" Albert yelled from within his house.

"Your neighbor," Kurt said. "I heard you were ill. Do you need any help?"

Albert opened his door and scowled at Kurt.

"I don't need any help from you!" he said. "Not from a goddamned Reinhart! Get off my property! Now! Or I'll call the sheriff!"

*****

Kurt had long since decided Albert's quarrel with his grandfather was a matter of their neighbor's invention.

Rauenthaler told people his one source of pride, his one achievement, his one reason for living as long as he had, came down to his not having lost his farm to Henry Reinhart.

No, he wasn't at all like those other worthless farmers—the Hagenbachs, Riegels, Lindens, Warners and Boeckers—who'd let that land-grabbing rascal take their farms. Albert boasted in Kensington he'd not only stayed away from alcohol and every other vice for the last forty-four years. He'd also kept himself free of debt. And there was only one reason for his choosing to lead such a model life.

"I made up my mind," he'd say, his voice rising on Main Street, "I'd do everything I could to keep my farm out of the grasp of Henry Reinhart. Since that time, I've never let down my guard. And that's why I still own my land—and he doesn't."

*****

Albert Rauenthaler's situation should've worked in Henry's favor. After all, Albert was an eighty-year-old single man who couldn't live forever, and he had no children, grandchildren or other relatives to leave his property to.

If he died without a will, Lafayette County would become the owner of his property by law. When the county auctioned it off, Henry would surely bid more for it than anybody else who wished to own it.

If Albert died with a will, no one could blame his legatees if they chose to split the large amount of money Henry would pay them for an otherwise unremarkable eighty-acre property with a dilapidated house and barn sitting on it.

Albert was well aware of the problem he faced and spoke of it often. He found many a willing ear—and almost unanimous support in his struggle to keep his farm out of the hands of his rapacious neighbor. But what good would it do him?

His adversary had committed fraud, arson and murder to acquire six of the farms in the section he was determined to own in its entirety. Nobody doubted he'd do whatever he had to do to get his hands on the seventh and last of those farms.

*****

Albert's falling ill gave his many supporters a great scare.

But when he drove down Main Street in Kensington in his 1931 Buick a few days after Kurt's unwelcome visit and walked into the grocery store looking the way he ordinarily did, his partisans breathed a collective sigh of relief.

All he'd had was some sort of bug, he told them. The penicillin the doctor had prescribed had worked its usual miracle. The community felt free again to scoff at Henry Reinhart's section-owning obsession.

Albert showed everybody he saw a letter he'd received from an Edinburgh attorney.

Henry Reinhart, the attorney had written, would give Albert the same deal for his farm he'd given the Boeckers for theirs. Albert would receive the same amount of money, and he could also live in his home as long as he wished.

His Grandfather's House

Kurt wondered why Albert didn't just accept the offer—and be damned glad his neighbor wanted his land so badly. Kurt had assumed he'd have to do the same housework for Albert he'd done for Edna.

Albert, though, had another idea. He stood in the middle of Main Street in Kensington with traffic stopped in both directions and a Saturday afternoon crowd assembled as if for a carnival. He held the lawyer's letter in one hand and a lit match in the other.

"Burn the letter, Albert!" the onlookers yelled. "Burn that damned letter!"

After he touched the flame to the paper, the crowd gave him a loud, gratifying cheer.

*****

During the following week, though, the merriment once again turned to gloom.

The doctor had called Albert back to his office. Some tests had to be done. The hospital in Edinburgh could do them. They'd take three days, maybe four. Albert would have to stay overnight in a hospital for the first time in his life.

The doctor wouldn't tell Albert what he suspected might be wrong with him.

But he had said, "It looks serious, Albert. Yes, it does look serious."

"It must be my heart," Albert told the grocer's teenage granddaughter working the cash register the next Saturday morning. "My dad keeled over one day and died. His ticker gave out just like that. And he was only seventy-three. He wasn't as big as I am either. The doctor says I should lose fifty pounds at least. You better take those doughnuts back. I should get to my car."

The grocer's granddaughter pushed the doughnuts away with tears in her eyes.

"Now, now, now," Albert soothed. "Everything's going to be all right. You'll see. I shouldn't be talking about my medical problems. You forget I said anything about them. Okay?"

*****

Albert went to the hospital in Edinburgh the next Monday. The following Thursday a surgeon removed a tumor from his colon. The operation took five hours, and Albert lost a lot of blood. Kensington assumed he wouldn't come out of the hospital alive. The tumor was malignant.

Albert remained in the hospital for six weeks. He didn't die, but he did run up substantial bills for his stay there as well as for the services of his doctor and the surgeon his doctor had called in to remove the tumor.

Albert had liked to brag about his humble, pinchpenny ways.

"That's why I don't owe anything to anybody," he'd add.

But now Albert's many well-wishers discovered he'd taken his frugality to the point of declining to purchase medical insurance. Kurt's grandfather bought the catastrophic kind for his family. And even though they'd never had to use it, Henry still considered it a bargain.

Albert also had to admit his checking and savings accounts at the Kensington State Bank held nowhere near enough money for him to make more than a small down payment on his medical bills.

He'd given up farming in the late 1930s. He'd sold his cows, horses and machinery. Since then, he'd collected rent from a farmer who lived across the road and grew crops on his land. In most of those years, though, the rent hadn't exceeded the money he'd spent on groceries and coal.

Thank God, he liked to say, television was free—at least after the cash he'd laid out for the set and the antenna on his roof. Like Elaine and Arny, he ate his meals, as well as his snacks in between, glued to it.

The people who'd saved his life, though, had to be compensated for their efforts. If the hospital and doctors filed suits against Albert, he'd have no defense. If they foreclosed on their judgment liens, the court would order the sheriff to sell his eighty acres. No one doubted the successful buyer would be Henry.

The time had come for Albert to swallow his pride and see Chester Smith about getting a mortgage loan on his farm.

*****

Kensingtonians knew Chester and Henry had settled their dispute over "that nasty business with the Boeckers," but they still seemed to despise one another.

Henry had left his money in Chester's bank—for his and his family's convenience only, he told Kurt. But Henry and Chester never spoke, not even when they passed one another on Main Street. The Smith-Reinhart alliance against the Riegels, Lindens and Warners, secret at the time, was a thing of the past. In Albert's case, Chester publicly opposed Henry.

Chester said a mortgage loan would be nothing more than a stopgap. He told Albert what he needed was a plan to keep Henry off the Rauenthaler farm forever.

And Chester had such a plan.

In the summer of 1956, the county had widened and blacktopped the gravel road that ran past Rauenthaler's house. It connected the blacktopped county line road on the west to the blacktopped road on the east leading north to Kensington and Edinburgh. Chester had learned a real estate developer from Chicago was interested in buying farmland in Kensington township. He'd subdivide the property and build reasonably priced homes for the workers who'd be moving into the area to fill jobs in the new farm implement factory going up on the south side of Edinburgh. He'd pay extra for land with access to a blacktopped road.

Chester asked if the developer would consider Albert's almost perfectly flat land, none of it in a floodplain. Through his lawyer in Chicago, the developer offered to pay three hundred fifty dollars an acre for it. Albert, though, wanted what Henry had offered to pay him—four hundred fifty dollars an acre.

The developer agreed but attached a condition to his offer. The county board would need to rezone the land so that it could be used for residential as well as agricultural purposes.

Albert, guided by Chester, accepted the developer's terms. How could he not? The deal would put an end to Henry's dream of owning the whole section. If the developer built two or three hundred houses on Albert's property, not even Henry could buy and tear them all down. No matter how inexpensive the dwellings were, it would cost millions to restore the acreage to farmland. Paved streets would be laid, water and sewage pipes buried, and utility lines strung.

Why, Chester asked, should Albert be the one to stand in the way of progress like that?

Chapter Twenty-One

In the third week of February of 1957, Chester Smith, who was said to have contributed significant amounts of money to the campaigns of the members of the Lafayette County board, all of them Republican, accompanied Albert to a meeting of the board in Edinburgh. Albert's rezoning petition was the only matter on the board's agenda that evening.

Chester had chosen a dozen other residents of Kensington township to speak in favor of Albert's request. One of them was the Reverend Cecil Crosley.

They never mentioned their desire to stymie Henry Reinhart. They emphasized rather, and at great length, the economic benefits the real estate development would bring to the Kensington community.

"And indeed," Chester argued when it was his turn to speak, "to the entire county."

Cecil closed the arguments for the rezoning petition by assuring the board that if Jesus Christ sat among them, "He'd surely cast his vote for Albert!"

The president of the board announced that only one person, Henry, had signed the sheet at the door indicating his wish to speak against the petition.

Chester and Cecil looked at one another and grinned like grade school boys. They were pleased with themselves. They had Henry right where they wanted him—thwarted, blocked.

Henry, who attended the meeting with Kurt, rose from his chair, peered around the room at Chester and his other opponents and scowled. He raised his arm and pointed at the members of the board, who sat behind a row of desks on a platform.

They stared back at him warily, as if they worried the long, gnarled index finger he aimed at them might somehow metamorphose into his notorious shotgun.

"We farm the land in Kensington township," he began. "If the people in Edinburgh want a new factory employing five hundred workers, the houses for those workers should be built in Edinburgh as well. Putting up hundreds of houses on eighty acres in a farming township like Kensington is insane. Think of all the traffic moving through our quiet village as those factory workers go to and from their jobs every day."

He paused to scrutinize his neighbors. They refused to look back at him.

He turned to the members of the board again.

"This idiotic developer from Chicago doesn't need to take our farmland and destroy it," he said. "There's room here in Edinburgh township for the houses he proposes to build. We have enough houses in Kensington township already. Putting up hundreds more on Albert Rauenthaler's flat, rich land is the most foolish goddamned idea I've ever heard of. You know that as well as I do. You can vote for what some big-city, big-bucks fool wants. Or you can vote for what you know in your hearts is right—Albert's eighty acres should be farmland forever."

With those few words, Henry was done. He sat down.

Kurt looked at their neighbors. They all turned away from him. Kurt could tell they knew his grandfather was right.

Arny and Elaine had heard talk about how cheap the houses would be. Which led to the inevitable question, "What sort of people will buy them?"

Arny and Elaine had chosen not to attend the rezoning proceeding.

"We'll only be humiliated," Elaine told Kurt.

Without any discussion among themselves, the board took a vote. As the president called out the names of the members, some looked Henry in the eye and barked out their yes vote. Some chose to gaze elsewhere and whisper theirs. In any event, they unanimously voted in favor of Albert's petition.

*****

The next evening at the dining room table, Kurt asked the question he felt he could put off no longer. Why had his grandfather doubted the neighbors were correct in concluding that Albert, Gus Hagenbach and Conrad Reinhart were guilty of nothing more than excessive drinking when they got together at Albert's house?

Henry looked up from his papers and glared at his grandson.

"I know what they did," he replied, his teeth clenched.

"How do you know what they did?"

126

"They asked me to join them."

That reply appeared to startle the grandfather who'd made it as much as it did the grandson who'd invited it.

The grandson, sensing he'd discovered pay dirt, pulled himself together again and pressed on.

"Albert said they never invited another man to their gatherings."

Henry scoffed. "Albert lied about that."

"When did this happen? How old were you?"

"I was eighteen. It was in the summer of the year I finished high school. Conrad took me along with him one night. They had all the curtains closed. The only light was from some candles they'd lit. They told me what they did, besides drinking, when they got together."

"What was that?"

Henry closed his eyes and shook his head.

Kurt persisted. "What did they do? Why did they have the curtains closed?"

"They told me they were doing that crime against nature stuff."

"Did you find that offensive? Did you resent being asked to join them?"

"No. Not at all. I didn't give a damn what they did. I told them that. But I also let them know I wasn't interested in it myself."

"Do you know why they singled you out?"

Henry continued to look across the table at his tenacious thirteen-year-old grandson as if he faced an inquisitor who'd threatened torture if he didn't spill his guts.

"I've always assumed," Henry replied, "they thought I was one of them. I wasn't an Eric Larson. I wasn't chasing after women as if my life depended on it."

"Weren't they afraid you'd tell other people what they told you?"

"You're damned right they were. But I had no wish to say anything about it to anybody else. You're the only person I've ever told. I'd heard about that law you found in the library. But they did what they did in private. They were adults. They weren't harming other people. It's another stupid law. My father convinced me of that a long time ago."

Kurt couldn't take his eyes off his grandfather.

"I promised them," Henry continued, "I'd never tell anybody what they were doing. That wasn't good enough for them, though."

"What do you mean?"

"They told me what would happen to me if I told other people what they did."

"What would happen to you?"

"They'd kill me."

Kurt gasped. "They told you they'd kill you?"

"They said I'd never testify against them in court. They'd take care of it the first time I opened my mouth. They'd kill me."

"Your own brother threatened to kill you?"

"He did. In some ways, though, I don't blame them for threatening me. They told me about a man in Edinburgh who got convicted for doing what they were doing. He went to prison, and within a week he was dead."

"What happened to him?"

"Some of the other inmates murdered him. They hung him up in his cell to make it look like a suicide. Nobody got punished for it, though. None of the inmates would talk about it."

Henry looked down at the newspaper in front of him.

Kurt, on the other hand, wasn't done. "If you were eighteen, Conrad must've been over fifty."

"He was."

"Was he planning to do things with you?"

Henry looked up from his paper again as if he were in pain.

"God, no," he said. "We were brothers. They'd invited me there for Albert. He was quite a bit younger than those other two."

Kurt no longer bothered to conceal how much he enjoyed his grandfather's disclosures.

"Albert found you attractive the way I do Eric Larson? He was in love with you?"

Kurt could tell from the agonized look on his grandfather's face he wouldn't get any answers to those questions.

But Kurt couldn't resist asking more. "Albert's still pissed because you weren't in love with him? Is that why he hates you?"

Henry peered at his grandson with narrowed eyes.

"Albert hates me," he said, "for the same reason everybody else does. He thinks I killed my brother, forged a will, burned down a neighbor's barn and swindled some other people out of their property. There's nothing I can say or do to prove my innocence in any of those things. That's just the way life is. But why should it matter to me what they think, as long as they don't lock me up in a jail or strap me down in an electric chair?"

Kurt had no response to those remarks.

"I should've kept my mouth shut about those men," his grandfather said. "Please don't tell anybody else what I've told you. It happened fifty years ago. Nobody needs to know about it now. All that stuff is over and done with."

Kurt wasn't so certain. "Is it?" he asked.

Chapter Twenty-Two

On a Friday morning late in March of 1957, the lawyer for the buyer of Albert's farm came out from Chicago to Kensington. He and Chester Smith's lawyer, who represented Albert but charged him no fee, closed the deal in Chester's office. Albert ended up holding in his hand a certified check for almost thirty-five thousand dollars.

Chester, having obtained the Reverend Cecil Crosley's promise not to let Albert out of his sight for a moment, gave him an hour to show the check around town. While Cecil proclaimed the deal God's gift to a Christian community, storekeepers and their clerks marveled at the amount of money the piece of paper stood for. By noon the check was back at the Kensington State Bank safely deposited in Albert's account, and Chester breathed a sigh of relief.

*****

That night Kurt's grandfather went to bed when he always did—as soon as he'd finished listening to the late news on the radio.

In the three years Henry had lived in his father's house on the hill, after Bertha's death had prompted him to make the move with Kurt, he hadn't sullied it with a television. The radio and the *Chicago Tribune* were more than sufficient for him to learn all he needed to know about the weather and the folly of the individuals currently running the world.

Eisenhower had at least proven, during his reelection campaign the previous autumn, he knew how to avoid wars America had no need to fight, one in Eastern Europe and another in the Middle East. Henry voted for him.

Whenever Arny or Elaine mentioned a program they'd seen on television, Henry gave them the kind of look devout members of Reverend Crosley's congregation would bestow upon a person who used a vulgar word to describe a sexual organ or activity in their presence.

Pretending to go to bed himself, Kurt went upstairs. But there was no possibility he'd sleep that Friday night. Standing at a north-facing window, he could see the leafless, black limbs of the oaks marching up the slope from the creek like a besieging army. The moon was almost full, and not a cloud blemished the sky.

Good, he thought. He wouldn't need a flashlight.

He could make out Albert Rauenthaler's house and barn on the section line road a mile away. He didn't have to see the fences that enclosed Rauenthaler's eighty-acre rectangle of land thrust into his grandfather's section like the head of an ax. He knew where they were.

*****

With one shoe in each hand, Kurt tiptoed down the back stairs. He paused in the kitchen and listened.

His grandfather slept on a daybed next to a nightstand in the room that used to be Otto's parlor. A couch and two stuffed chairs from that era remained in place.

Kurt was certain his grandfather was sound asleep by then, as he almost always was at that hour, and hadn't heard him coming down the stairs.

On a line of hooks near the back doorway, and on the floor below the hooks, Kurt and his grandfather kept the outer garments, gloves and boots they wore when they worked outside in cold weather.

Kurt grabbed his army surplus cap with the flaps that came down over his ears, two sweatshirts smelling a bit too much like the barn, a tattered coat that would last him until spring, a pair of eight-buckle rubber boots, and his work gloves.

Out on the back steps in the cold night air, he wasted no time wrapping himself in his clothes and pulling on his boots.

He ran down the hill toward the barn. In the toolshed, he found what he needed without turning on a light—a claw bar.

He hurried farther down the hill, waded the creek, which was low for March, and climbed the bank on the other side.

After that, he walked as fast as he could through the woods and between two long rows of bent-over corn stalks to Albert's farm.

*****

A half mile of fence on the west boundary of Albert's land, a quarter mile on the south and another half mile on the east separated the Reinhart and Rauenthaler farms. The fence consisted of woven wire topped with two strands of barbed wire attached to wooden posts with steel staples the size of a grown person's thumb.

His Grandfather's House

Ordinarily, it was the responsibility of adjoining neighbors to maintain half the length of their common fence. Henry and Albert, though, hadn't observed that custom since the day they began owning bordering farms, which was the day Otto Reinhart died.

Forty-six years later, though, what did it matter?

Albert, who'd owned no livestock for the last twenty years, had no need to keep up his fences.

Henry pastured his cattle and hogs in his creek land and woods, surrounded on all sides by fencing he and his family maintained on such a regular basis it gave the livestock no chance to escape. He wasn't about to repair the fences between his land and that of a neighbor he intended to dispossess anyway.

So on the boundary lines separating their farms, Albert and Henry had let the posts rot and the wires between them sag. Although the fences would've been no barrier to wandering livestock like the Boeckers' hungry cows, they accomplished one thing. Every time they forced Kurt to turn around when he plowed for corn, mowed hay or spread manure, they underscored for him Albert's absurd intransigence.

*****

Kurt attacked the posts with his claw bar. Their old, dry wood readily gave up the staples somebody years ago—a youthful Henry or Albert maybe—had hammered into them.

Kurt still had to pull the fencing away from the posts. Several summers of withered morning glories clung to the wires like the frozen fingers of the dead.

Kurt rolled the barbed wire in hoops and the woven wire in cylinders. He put the staples in a gunnysack he'd brought with him.

He threw his arms around the posts, working them back and forth and side to side. The frost had gone out of the ground early that March. Every post he encountered eventually gave itself up to him with a wet, sucking sound.

*****

By sunrise Saturday morning, Kurt had taken down all the fence on the west and south sides of Rauenthaler's property and most of it on the east side.

He was working his way north toward Albert's house and barn.

He'd left heaps of rusted wire and piles of rotted posts behind him.

The sudden light streaking across the prairie startled him. He straightened himself up from his work and peered at Albert's buildings, which were as pink as Bertha's peonies in May. As tired as he was, he was also damned glad he'd spent the night removing fence.

Emil Olson's two-ton truck was parked in the driveway outside Albert's back door. Neighbors had come over Friday afternoon and loaded it with the few possessions Albert had worth giving to the poor. This job hadn't required Emil's semitrailer.

Albert was to sleep in his own bed one last night.

Chester Smith had arranged for him to move into the new home for old people in Edinburgh, to which Albert would take only his clothes, personal items and television. Those things would easily fit within the trunk and backseat of Chester's Cadillac.

The canvas tarpaulin covering the back of Emil's truck and the possessions Albert was giving away had been an unnecessary precaution. The day for Albert's move was going to be bright and sunny.

Kurt had less than a dozen posts left to pull when he saw, out of the corner of his eye, his grandfather's Pontiac coming up the road on the east side of the section.

Henry hadn't bothered to wake Arny and Elaine after he'd discovered his grandson was missing that morning. Instead he looked toward Albert's farm from the house on the hill and saw the mounds of posts and wire where the fences had been.

Now he parked his car on the side of the road and walked across a cornfield to help his grandson finish removing the posts.

*****

After Albert had fallen ill the previous autumn, Henry accompanied a truckload of cattle to the stockyards in Chicago. He'd told Elaine and Arny he wanted to make sure the commission agent got the highest possible price for his livestock. But Kurt knew his grandfather, who drove his own car and didn't ride with Emil in his truck, had another reason to travel to Chicago that day. After the cattle were sold, he went to the Loop to see a lawyer.

He brought home a package of papers and spread them out on the dining room table. He spent the entire evening, from supper—a beef stew Kurt had made with onions, carrots and turnips from the garden he'd inherited from Otto and Bertha—to bedtime, on one activity. He read the documents from the law firm and signed them. Edna Boecker hadn't taken so long with her papers that winter day in her kitchen.

Kurt's grandfather drove to Edinburgh the next morning to mail the papers back to the law firm in Chicago. He was taking no chances on the people who worked in the post office in Kensington.

"They're all too goddamned nosy," he said.

That evening, finishing the stew with oat bread Kurt had baked following Bertha's recipe, Henry looked across the supper table at his grandson and pointed in the direction of the house at the bottom of the hill.

"Don't tell them what we've been up to," he said.

Kurt shook his head to indicate he wouldn't consider doing such a thing.

"They talk too damned much," Henry said. "They'd let everybody in Kensington know our business. And we sure as hell don't want that now."

Chapter Twenty-Three

K urt pulled on a post not quite as rotten as the others. When his grandfather pulled on it with him, it came slipping out of the early-spring mud with a sound like a sigh.

Then they heard a familiar voice from Albert's back porch.

"What's going on out here?"

Albert, always an early riser after what he called his drinking years, had caught them two posts short of completing the task Kurt had begun the night before.

Albert carefully made his way down his back porch steps, bent over and shaking in the cold morning air, still looking haggard from his illness, surgery and old age. Hatless, he negotiated the bottom step and looked in their direction, squinting his eyes and shielding them from the bright sun with his cupped hands. He stumbled across his backyard toward the intruders.

"Reinhart!" he yelled when he was close enough to recognize his neighbors. "What are you doing here? You goddamned thief! You murdering son of a bitch! Get off my property!"

"It isn't your property anymore," Henry replied.

"It isn't yours either!" Albert shouted back, charging toward them. "Get out, I said!"

He came within twenty feet of his neighbors and saw they were standing their ground. He stopped and stared at them, contemplating his next move.

"My grandson likes to work at night," Henry said, sweeping his arm in the direction of the fields Albert had still owned when he'd risen from his bed the previous day. "So now, look. All the fences that used to separate our farms are gone."

Albert turned toward the fields he'd sold. A puzzled expression came over his weary face.

"Why did you do that?" he asked Kurt.

"They were in our way, Albert," Henry said. "Just like you, they were in our way. We had to get rid of them."

"You had no right to do that!" Albert exploded again. "That developer from Chicago might've wanted those fences left where they were. You had no right to take them out. I'll call Chester Smith. He'll let the developer's lawyer know what you've done. You've gone too far this time, Henry Reinhart. You'll answer to the law for this!"

Albert turned toward the house he'd lived his entire life in.

"Go ahead and call Chester," Kurt's grandfather said to his neighbor's back. "When he talks to that lawyer in Chicago, he'll find out I've got the right to do anything I want with the fences my grandson took down. Go ahead and call Chester."

Albert turned and looked at Henry. "What in hell do you mean by that?"

"I mean," Henry replied, "you're standing on my property. I own these eighty acres now. They're mine. This whole section is mine."

Albert studied Henry's face as if he'd never seen him before.

"You've taken leave of your senses," Albert said. "You're insane. Everybody says you're insane."

He glanced at Kurt.

"Everybody says your whole family's insane."

Henry sneered at those remarks as if they were arguments the world was flat.

"I sold my property," Albert said, "to a developer from Chicago. He paid me good money for my farm. He's going to put up houses here. That'll keep you off my land forever."

Henry shook his head and laughed. "No, Albert. The money you received for your farm was my money."

"Bullshit!" Albert yelled. "I'd never take your money for nothing! You killed your own brother to get your money! I don't need your goddamned money!"

Henry laughed again. "There was no developer from Chicago who wanted your farm, Albert. You took my money for your property."

Albert's mouth hung open. "You'd better not be right! Before I'd leave this farm and let you have it, I'd kill you!"

"Go into your house," Henry said, "and call Chester Smith. You and your friends think the lawyer who came out here and gave you your check worked for some developer in Chicago. That lawyer works for me. I paid him to close the deal with you. Get Chester on your phone. Maybe he knows the truth already. I asked my lawyer to call him this morning and tell him I own your farm. Maybe he's already done it."

"I signed a deed!" Albert was yelling again. "The deed didn't say I sold my farm to you! Your name wasn't on it!"

"You sold your farm to a bank in Chicago," Henry said. "You didn't pay attention. The bank was only a trustee. It holds title to your farm in a land trust. I'm the beneficiary of that trust. On Monday, my

138

lawyer and the bank in Chicago will put the title to your eighty acres in my name. Go call the bank, Albert. Call Chester. Call my lawyer. Call anybody you please. The only thing you'll find out is the truth. I tricked you. I tricked Chester Smith. I tricked everybody. You forced me to do it. I offered you a better deal than you got. You would've received the same amount of money, but you could've stayed here in your home for the rest of your life. You chose to burn that offer on Main Street in Kensington. But now I own your land, and you can't do a goddamned thing about it. It's all as legal as it can be."

Albert's face bore the horrified expression of a person who'd witnessed a brutal murder. He turned and walked as fast as he could up the steps to his back porch and into his house.

He'd inherited his farm from his parents when he was still in his youth. He'd spent most of his life thereafter keeping the farm out of the hands of Henry Reinhart. Had he failed?

*****

Kurt and his grandfather finished their work. The fence that used to separate Albert's farm from Henry's was gone. The junkman would come down from Edinburgh to pick up the wire. The wind would dry out the posts, and the Reinharts would saw them into sections and burn them in their furnaces.

A car turned off the road into Albert's driveway. The neighbor who'd spoken most passionately before the county board in favor of the rezoning stopped his car when he saw Henry and his grandson halfway between what used to be Albert's barn and house. He kept his motor running and rolled down his window.

"Albert called me," he said.

Kurt could see the neighbor's hands trembling on his steering wheel.

"He told me what you've done," the neighbor said.

"Then you know," Kurt's grandfather said, "you're trespassing on my property. I'll let you stay only to help Albert remove himself and his possessions from it."

The neighbor opened and closed his mouth, but no words came out of it.

"Go help Albert," Henry said to the neighbor. "I'd appreciate it if you would. My grandson and I have a lot of work to get done here today."

*****

Albert, lugging a five-gallon gasoline can, came down the back porch steps. He crossed the backyard lopsided and headed straight for his barn.

Kurt, his grandfather and the neighbor, who was still in the safety of his car, watched Albert fumble at the rusty latch of the barn door.

"What's he doing?" the neighbor asked.

The answer came from within the house in the form of an explosion.

They turned and saw flames at the kitchen windows.

Kurt ran toward the barn.

Albert, having opened the door, turned and looked at Kurt.

"Give me that," Kurt yelled, pointing at the gasoline can.

Albert turned again and ran into the barn.

Kurt attempted to run after him, but his grandfather, proving how quick and strong he was at sixty-eight, threw his arms around his grandson's shoulders and held him back.

"Burn them down, Albert," Henry yelled. "We don't want your goddamned buildings. You're saving us the bother of tearing them down."

Albert came out of the barn without his gasoline can and looked at his house.

Flames escaped from it through its shattered kitchen windows and licked their way up its clapboard walls.

The neighbor got out of his car. His eyes danced from the house to the barn to the Reinharts to Albert and back again.

Like an outraged deity, white smoke from moldy hay and straw squeezed through the cracks in the walls of Albert's barn.

Henry laughed. "You've done the right thing, Albert. You should be proud of yourself. These buildings are worthless. We'll farm the land they're standing on."

Albert scowled. "Your own brother wanted to murder you. I wish he'd done it."

His Grandfather's House

He hurried across the backyard again, this time to his car. He kept it in a side yard next to a sagging chicken coop. Arny and Elaine had heard in Kensington he'd sold the car, as a collector's item, to somebody from Edinburgh who'd come to get it on moving day.

Steam boiled up from the cellar door above the steps that led down to the basement of the house. The water pipes had burst.

The dry barn behind Kurt and his grandfather was in flames. Kurt could feel the heat through his sweatshirts and coat.

Albert pressed his gas pedal to the floor, his car aimed at Henry and his nasty grandson, the boy who'd had the sass to tell a Christian minister what he was saying from his pulpit was bullshit.

Kurt and his grandfather, surprised by their elderly neighbor's aggression, took off running again.

Albert swung his steering wheel but not fast enough. He missed them both.

Kurt could see, as the car sped past him, Albert was clutching his chest.

Albert crashed through the burning wall of the barn like the daredevil at the Lafayette County Fair in Edinburgh who drove a car through a hoop of flames.

The neighbor jumped up and down.

"No, Albert!" he screamed. "No!"

Albert's car plowed into the barn, hit a hayloft post head-on and stalled.

Kurt and his grandfather ran into the barn through the hole in the wall the car had made.

Albert was slumped against the steering wheel, his head bleeding.

Kurt pried open the car door, put his arms around Albert and pulled him out.

Dodging embers falling down from above, Kurt and his grandfather positioned themselves on either side of Albert with their shoulders under his armpits. They dragged him out of the barn, took him to the neighbor's car and laid him on the backseat.

The neighbor stared at Albert.

"Get moving!" Henry barked. "Get him to the hospital in Edinburgh as fast as you can. Go!"

Chapter Twenty-Four

K urt and his grandfather could hear the volunteer fire truck coming down from Kensington. They could hear cars speeding toward what used to be Albert Rauenthaler's farm but now without fences around it and its buildings in flames.

The neighbor turned and looked at the cars arriving in both directions on the new blacktop road. He turned and looked at Henry and Kurt. Caught in a seizure of indecision, he turned and turned again.

"What are you waiting for?" Henry yelled. "Do you want me to drive your car?"

Reluctant, frightened, the neighbor got into his car and backed it the length of the driveway. At the road he met the first of the other neighbors to arrive.

After a brief discussion, he got out of his car.

The young woman who'd played Lady Macbeth a few years back took his place behind the wheel and sped off toward Edinburgh.

More neighbors and residents of Kensington, parking their cars along the side of the road, came running toward the burning house and barn.

The first neighbor remained at the entrance to the driveway. Gesticulating in the direction of Kurt and his grandfather, he loudly told everybody who came past him what had happened and why the house and barn were on fire.

"Henry tricked Albert into selling him his farm! There was no developer! Albert went nuts! He set his buildings on fire! He tried to kill Henry and his grandson!"

The fire truck pulled into the driveway. Although its presence caused a great deal of yelling and running back and forth on the part of the spectators, no firefighting ensued.

Before any further effort was wasted, the fire chief thought to ask Henry if he wanted the volunteers to attempt to put the fires out.

"Hell, no," Henry replied, as expressionless as the bronze bust of a victorious general. "Let them burn to the ground."

The sheriff and a number of his deputies showed up in their cars with their sirens wailing and lights flashing.

The publisher and a photographer from the *Edinburgh Times* were close behind them.

Far down the road at the end of the long lines of cars parked on either side of it, Chester Smith and Cecil Crosley got out of Chester's

Cadillac. Kurt watched as the two of them began walking toward the fiery scene.

When they reached the driveway, Kurt and a deputy who'd been Kensington High's quarterback in his junior and senior years two and three autumns ago greeted them.

"His grandfather," the deputy said, "doesn't want either of you on his property. If you come any closer, I'll have to arrest you."

Chester and Cecil chose to stay where they were, glaring at a boy in dirty clothes blowing his nose and wiping his eyes on his coat sleeve.

When Gwendolyn Smith showed up and saw Kurt, she burst into tears herself and hugged him as if she were his mother.

"They told me," she said, "you could've been killed."

The next day, which was a Sunday, Kurt's shabby clothes and smudged, unsmiling face appeared in a photograph of him and his grandfather on the first page of the *Edinburgh Times*. They stood in front of the flames consuming what was left of Albert's barn.

"FIERY TRAGEDY ENDS NEIGHBORS' FEUD" was the headline above the photo. The publisher himself wrote the story below it.

The same photograph with similar headlines appeared on the front pages of the Chicago newspapers that Sunday. The reporters quoted the publisher of the *Edinburgh Times* at length. After all, he'd spent forty-five years of his life working on the story.

*****

Albert Rauenthaler was dead on arrival at the Edinburgh Community Hospital.

The doctors decided he must've suffered a heart attack. They gave cardiac arrest as the cause of his death.

Albert had executed a will the same day he signed the contract to sell his farm. In the will he left everything he owned—which, when he died, was the money he'd received from Henry for his farm—to the same legatee Edna Boecker had chosen, the Edinburgh Community Hospital.

The *Edinburgh Times* noted that at least Albert, unlike the Boeckers, had some connection to the hospital. He owed it and its owners, for saving his life, a substantial part of what his will gave it.

*****

By the third Sunday in May of 1957, even with the addition of Albert's eighty acres to their farm, the Reinharts had finished their planting.

Arny and Elaine baked pies with the rhubarb Kurt had picked for them. They were also roasting beef and making ice cream for a birthday party for Kurt that evening. Henry had promised them he'd attend.

Kurt and his grandfather spent most of the day digging up soil in a swampy area down by the creek. They used the black earth to top off the holes where the basement of Albert's house and the foundation of his barn had been. They had to fill the manure spreader several times to get the job done.

"I found out something I should tell you," Henry said, without interrupting his work. "But nobody else needs to know anything about it."

Kurt, fourteen now, had added three inches to his height in the last year. His shoulders had broadened, too, but his waist and hips had remained narrow. Elaine said he looked more like Johnny every day.

He emptied his spade in the manure spreader and turned to his grandfather.

"When I saw the lawyer in Chicago on Friday," Henry said, "he told me an interesting story."

Kurt, his grandfather and Arny had worked late into the night on Thursday, which was actually Kurt's birthday, and finished the planting. During the predicted Friday morning rain, Henry took the train to Chicago to pay the lawyer his final bill and obtain the deed to Albert's farm and all the other legal papers concerning the purchase he might need in the future.

"After my lawyer and Chester Smith's lawyer closed the deal that day in March," Henry said, "they had lunch together in Edinburgh and some drinks to wash it down. Smith's lawyer said Chester had suspected all along I was posing as the developer who wanted to buy Albert's land."

"All along?" Kurt asked. "He suspected all along?"

"That's what my lawyer said."

"Before the rezoning hearing? He knew it was a sham?"

"He'd guessed it was meant to convince Albert and the people a developer seriously intended to build houses on his land."

"He saw through the whole damned thing."

Henry emptied his spade in the manure spreader and remained silent.

"What made Chester think," Kurt asked, "you were posing as the developer?"

"When he found out the offer to buy the property was from that bank in Chicago acting as a trustee."

"He suspected you were using the bank to hide your identity?"

"That's right. The same way I'd used his bank so my foolish neighbors wouldn't know they were borrowing money from a man who'd murdered his brother, burned down his neighbor's barn and forged his father's will."

"But Chester didn't tell Albert or anybody else what he thought you were doing."

"Why would he? He and his doctor friends were going to get my dough. Why would he want to see the deal fall apart?"

"God, what a crook that bastard is."

Henry laughed. "We already knew that."

"He betrayed Albert. He betrayed all the people backing him."

"And that's why my lawyer says we don't want anybody else to find out about this. The people might think I was in cahoots with Chester and his lawyer. They might ask the authorities to do something about it. The state's attorney could file a lawsuit. A judge could rule against us and throw the deal out. My cynical lawyer says you can never predict what might happen when the people get upset and demand the politicians do something to make them feel better."

"Even though you broke no law."

"My lawyer assured me I broke no law."

Chapter Twenty-Five

During their digging in the swamp, Kurt had a question for his grandfather.

"When the Hagenbach barn burned down, you told the *Edinburgh Times* reporter a tramp had set it on fire. Was that the truth?"

Again, Henry continued working. "I knew exactly what happened. Your grandmother gave that beggar food. She fed all of them who asked her politely and didn't appear to be too drunk. But she didn't know he was sleeping in her deceased father's barn. I did, and I knew he set fires in it to keep himself warm. I knew he was drinking, too."

"But you didn't tell anybody?"

"No, I didn't. It was Cousin Claude's property then. Your grandmother had written to him and offered to keep an eye on the farm for him until he and his family moved out from Chicago. He wrote back and told her he didn't want her or me to have anything to do with his property. Both of us should stay away from it."

"That's what the asshole told Grandma and you?"

"That's what he said. In writing. I was only following his wishes."

"The guy who set the fire—what happened to him?"

"That was the one time I violated Cousin Claude's rule. When I saw the smoke, I went into the barn. The poor fellow who'd set the fire was much younger than I'd thought he was. He was a kid, only a few years older than you are now."

Kurt stopped digging again and looked at his grandfather.

"He'd inhaled too much smoke," Henry said. "He was going to die in there. I picked him up and carried him out. I washed his face in the snow. I walked him to the road. I told him it was time for him to get away from that barn as fast as he could. He looked over my shoulder and saw the fire he'd started. He took my advice. He ran like hell. They never found him."

"You're telling me you didn't start the fire yourself? You just waited for him to do it? Some young guy Grandma felt sorry for and fed?"

"That's what I did. No matter what Gus thought of me, he should've left his farm to your grandmother. She'd worked damned hard over the years to keep her father and herself on the property. But I didn't commit any crime. I went to see a lawyer. He said I had every right to save that kid's life. He'd be willing to argue before a jury I didn't aid and abet an arsonist. He'd take the case all the way to the United States Supreme Court if he had to. I liked that lawyer a lot."

"Did you ever tell anybody else you saved the beggar's life?"

"Only the lawyer. He told me I had no obligation to reveal that information to anybody else, and it would be best for me if I didn't."

"You didn't tell Grandma?"

"Not even her."

Kurt dropped his spade and did something he'd never done before. He gave his startled grandfather a hug.

"I'm glad," Kurt said, "you got that guy out of the barn and let him run away."

*****

In September of that year, 1957, Kurt began high school.

One Sunday evening in the autumn, after two long weekend days Henry, Kurt and Arny had spent picking the last of the corn before the next rain came, Henry asked Kurt to make some entries in his account books. He complained that writing the figures in the narrow columns hurt his eyes.

Within a month, Kurt was keeping the accounts by himself. He also filled out his grandfather's 1040 income tax return in the following April.

Henry was impressed. Kurt showed him how he could take a deduction for the loss of Albert's house and barn and lower his tax bill.

Henry explained it to Elaine and Arny during their birthday supper for Kurt on the day he turned fifteen, which was May 16, 1958.

"Otherwise," he said, "we would've just pissed the money away to those idiots in Washington."

"What did you lose?" Elaine asked Henry. "I thought you intended to demolish Albert's buildings."

Henry laughed. "I did, but I could've changed my mind. Kurt says we could've taken our time with it. He and I could've moved into Albert's house while we had our house renovated. We could've filled Albert's barn with straw and hay, too. Kurt showed me the IRS rules. It's perfectly legal to do what we did. I owned the house and barn and other structures the day Albert set them on fire. That's all that matters."

His Grandfather's House

Whenever Kurt ate supper with Elaine and Arny, they always asked him to stay after the meal and watch television with them. Kurt did so the Friday evening he turned fifteen.

One fortunate aspect of watching television was that neither Kurt nor his hosts had to attempt conversation. By then, though, he found the lives of his uncle and aunt more interesting than whatever they chose to watch on television. He had questions for them he'd ask during the breaks for commercials.

He could see it mattered to Arny and Elaine that the people who knew them believed they were a happily married couple who, for whatever reason, couldn't have children.

But he also knew his aunt and uncle had never lived together as ordinary husbands and wives did. They'd dropped some pretenses. They'd had separate bedrooms and bathrooms from the time Kurt and Henry moved out of their house to live in the house on the hill.

"Do you really think," Kurt asked them during one commercial after the supper celebrating his fifteenth birthday, "Granddad murdered his brother?"

Arny grimaced. "Everybody says he did, Kurt."

Elaine laughed. "He got rid of his brother and sisters. He got rid of Bertha's cousin. He got rid of all those other silly neighbors. So what if it took forging a will, giving his brother a shove and setting a barn on fire to start the ball rolling? He got exactly what he wanted."

Kurt looked at Elaine without finding anything amusing in what she'd said.

"It doesn't bother you," he asked, "to live here with a murderer?"

Elaine scoffed. "I've never owned any land he needed to murder me for or cheat me out of. I've been a loyal member of his gang. I've never worried about what he might've done so many years ago nobody really cares anymore."

Kurt went through all of his grandfather's financial records. He soon had them compiled in a series of notebooks, a dozen altogether, each of which bore on its spine in ballpoint ink four years, which were

149

as recent as 1955 through 1958 and as remote as 1911 through 1914.

Henry couldn't conceal his delight. Nights at his end of the table, after he finished reading the *Chicago Tribune*, he'd immerse himself in the notebooks, fingering through them as if they were scripture.

From time to time, without looking up from the page to which he'd turned, he'd put a question to his grandson regarding an entry— but not because he doubted its accuracy. His purpose was to drive home to himself once again what he'd accomplished.

Before he went to bed, he'd perform one last ritual. He'd pick up the latest book containing the plat maps for Lafayette County. He'd turn to the page for Kensington township. There he'd see what he'd spent his adult life working for, the whole section with nothing within its four one-mile borders but his name, Henry Otto Reinhart, and three digits indicating the number of acres he owned, 640.

*****

After Albert Rauenthaler's death and the news of Henry Reinhart's latest brazen but successful legal chicanery, Kurt's classmates didn't know whether to ostracize him for siding with his grandfather or idolize him for surviving Albert's attempt to kill him and then heroically dashing into a burning barn to try to save his attacker's life.

The neighbor who'd witnessed what happened told the publisher of the *Edinburgh Times* Albert's car had come within inches of running down both of his intended victims.

At the beginning of Kurt's sophomore year in high school, the coach of the Kensington High football, basketball, baseball and track-and-field teams, along with the best athletes on those squads, asked him to play with them. His six-foot size and his strength and agility qualified him for all those sports, they told him, if only he'd practice more. They saw what he could do during the PE classes he was required to participate in.

Kurt thanked the coach for asking him to join the teams.

"But I've got work to do on my grandfather's farm," he said. "It's a lot of work. I'm sorry, but it won't leave me any time for organized sports."

"His crazy grandpa must not want him to play," the coach told the English teacher.

A classmate of Kurt's, Rodney Adenauer, had overheard their conversation. Rodney was positive the coach and the English teacher, both one year out of college, were in love.

The English teacher shook her head. "Kurt told me his grandfather said he was free to play any sport he wanted to play."

"So why isn't Kurt playing for us?" the coach asked.

"I think I can guess why," the English teacher replied, with a smirk. "Kurt loves reading books, lots of books. They and his farmwork might not leave him much time for sports."

Chapter Twenty-Six

Kurt and Arny were in the woods sawing and splitting a hickory blown down in a thunderstorm the previous year. It was the Friday after Thanksgiving in 1958.

Henry, seventy then, was making his third trip across the creek on his tractor pulling the hay wagon loaded with chopped wood. When he reached his destination, which would be one of his two houses, he'd toss the wood through an open basement window into the woodbin behind the furnace.

He'd soon be back for a fourth load and as many more as the short November day allowed. No matter how much money he had in the bank, he refused to pay for coal to heat his houses. He'd much rather use the free timber that grew on his land and fell in a storm.

"Did you know," Kurt asked his forty-five-year-old uncle, "Albert Rauenthaler preferred men to women?"

Arny looked at Kurt. "Some people used to wonder about that."

"And about Grandma's father, Gus, and Grandpa's brother, Conrad."

"Them, too. Nobody ever believed it was so."

Kurt brought his sledgehammer down on a wedge and split a section of hickory trunk in two.

"But it was," he said. "For all three of them, it was."

"How do you know that?" Arny asked.

"Somebody told me."

"Who told you?"

Kurt pointed the handle of his sledgehammer in the direction of the tractor and hay wagon disappearing behind the barn.

"Him," he replied. "They let him know they preferred men to women."

"He came right out and told you that?"

"He did."

"Why did they talk to him about it?"

"They asked him to join them. He was eighteen. He turned them down. Then they warned him, if he let anybody else know what they were doing, they'd kill him."

After hearing those disclosures, Arny left the head of his sledgehammer on the ground.

"He told you that?" he asked.

"That's what he told me," Kurt said, preparing another blow.

Arny waited until Kurt hit his target.

Then he looked at his nephew again. "Did he tell you about me?"

Kurt let the head of his sledgehammer rest on a section of the wood he'd split.

"Is there something he knows about you I don't?" he asked.

Arny, who'd claimed Vic Warner's weight problem was nothing compared to his own, was close to shedding tears.

"I prefer men to women," he said. "If that's the way you wish to put it. But I've never acted on that preference. Never. Not once. Not with anybody."

Kurt looked around. They'd chopped enough wood for two more hay wagon loads. They might've already sawn and split all the wood they'd need that afternoon.

"I see," Kurt said, gazing at his uncle again.

"I was a failure with Elaine from the first day we married," Arny said. "That's why we never had children."

"Elaine must've been disappointed."

"She wanted children. Two, she told me. A girl and a boy. But she wasn't disappointed in me. She never really wanted me for that sort of thing anyway."

"Then why did she marry you?"

"She thought she'd gotten too old for what she called romantic love. So I was worth taking a chance on."

Arny wiped his tears off his face with his bare hand.

"My father," he chose to add, "owned a big farm and had money in the bank."

"That's why she married you?"

"Yeah. And that's why she's still here. She doesn't give a damn what people say about us. I actually think she enjoys it. She loved it when you yelled and swore at Cecil during Mom's funeral."

Kurt pulled a handkerchief out of his pocket.

"I haven't used this yet," he said.

Arny took Kurt's offering and applied it to his face.

*****

The next two days of the Thanksgiving weekend were also supposed to be chilly but sunny. Kurt, Arny and Henry would easily fill the basement bins. A lot of the wood they'd saw and split that weekend they'd have to stack in piles outside the two houses.

Most of the neighbors laughed at them for burning wood instead of coal. They said it was far too much work. Kurt had decided those who were so easily amused would never comprehend why his grandfather now owned a section of land and had money in the bank—and they didn't.

Kurt and Arny sat on sections of the hickory trunk looking at one another.

"I didn't want to go off and fight in that damned war," Arny said. "I would've ended up dead, sure as hell. I wouldn't have been as lucky as Johnny was. Your granddad wanted me home here helping him with the farmwork. Elaine wanted me here for the same reason."

"I'm sure," Kurt said, "they also didn't want to see you dead or wounded."

Arnie made no response to that remark.

"Elaine and I offered to adopt you," he said. "Lorelei didn't take any interest in you. I was thirty by then. Johnny was in the army. Elaine and I thought if you were legally our son, maybe they wouldn't draft me. Dad agreed with us."

"Why didn't you do that?"

"Lorelei wouldn't let us. She was just being mean. She didn't care if I got drafted. She made senseless remarks. She said having you had ruined her figure. And that's why she wouldn't give you up. And Mom agreed with her. She said no mother should have her child taken away from her. Dad got mad at Mom and told her she didn't know what the fuck she was talking about. He said that in front of Elaine and me. Those were awful times for us, during that damned war. Knowing we might find out any day Johnny was dead. Knowing the news would break our hearts."

*****

Kurt could remember, when he was still quite young, people saying he was an orphan. His mother had run off, and his father had killed himself.

Lorelei and Johnny had both chosen to leave him behind with his Reinhart grandparents, uncle and aunt.

The son the two seventeen-year-olds had created in the backseat of Henry's 1936 Pontiac was among the least of their concerns.

Whenever Kurt thought about that, he realized how lucky he'd been.

*****

After Henry left to make his fourth trip of the afternoon across the creek with his hay wagon filled with wood as if he were Santa on his sleigh, Kurt turned to Arny.

"He knew you preferred men?" he asked his balding uncle. "Did you tell him?"

"I told him," Arny replied. "But it didn't make any difference to him. He acted as if he already knew."

"But you didn't have to fight in the war. They didn't draft you after all?"

"I got drafted. Even though Johnny had joined up, I got drafted. I was thirty-one years old. It was 1944. They needed everybody they could lay their hands on."

Arny wiped his eyes again with Kurt's handkerchief.

"We don't have to talk about this," Kurt said.

"No, no. It's all right. I'm glad we're talking about it."

Kurt and Arny sat down again on sections of the hickory trunk.

"It was one of the reasons Johnny enlisted," Arny said. "People thought it reduced my chances of getting drafted. I loved your father. We all did, even Elaine. I'm sorry he had to go through that war. Dad's right. The war was what killed him."

"Nobody ever told me you were drafted."

"Nobody ever knew I was drafted. Nobody except Elaine and Dad. We didn't even want Mom to know. We never told her. She never knew I preferred men."

"But you didn't have to fight. How did you get out of it?"

Arny looked at Kurt and shook his head. "It was the worst damned day of my life. I had to go to Chicago to report for duty. Dad took me there. He told Mom we were going down to Ottawa to look at some cattle for sale. He said we'd eat lunch in a restaurant along the way."

Arny used Kurt's handkerchief to blow his nose.

156

"I'm sorry," he said.

"Don't worry about it. Throw it in the wash. Keep it."

"Dad and Elaine were as scared as I was I'd have to go off and fight. They knew I'd get killed. Elaine was taking care of you and doing almost all the housework. Mom was sitting up in Lorelei's room playing rummy with her. Dad couldn't do the outside work all by himself."

"How did you get out of it?" Kurt asked.

Arny, shaking his head again, looked at Kurt.

"This is the worst of it," he said. "I did what Elaine and Dad told me to do."

"What was that?" Kurt asked, softly, as if he hadn't already guessed.

"I told those people I was homosexual. It was the word Elaine and Dad said I should use. I also told them I'd never done anything with another man, and I never intended to. But that didn't make any difference to those guys. They told me to get my ass out of there. They never wanted to see me again. One of them told me he hoped I'd die a slow, agonizing death when I got to prison for molesting a boy."

"Jesus, that's the way they talked to you?"

"I told them I'd never molest a boy. They told me to shut my mouth. They'd heard all they needed to hear. They didn't want to be in the same room with me another second. When I left, I could hear them calling me a queer and a faggot."

"I'm sorry," Kurt said, wiping his own eyes with the sleeve of his coat. "I'm sorry you had to go through that. I'm sorry those people treated you the way they did."

"Thank you, Kurt. You're a good boy. You've always been a good boy. And your own mother wanted to get rid of you with a coat hanger. I'm damned glad that never happened."

"Yeah, me too."

Part Three

Kurt, Sixteen to Eighteen

1959-1961

Chapter Twenty-Seven

Gwendolyn Smith had a furnished coach house she rented to students attending Northern Illinois University in DeKalb. The house was in the woods behind the Smiths' main residence.

The student, so the story went, often came out ahead. He—the student was always a male—worked as a part-time teller at the Kensington State Bank. If he put in enough hours, his wages could exceed his rent.

Gwendolyn seemed to let physical attraction play a large part in her choice of a tenant.

The student who moved into Gwendolyn's coach house on Labor Day in 1959 was, according to the girls in Kurt's junior class at Kensington High, "the cutest of them all."

A few days later, Kurt met him. Kurt was at the bank to deposit checks and withdraw cash for his grandfather. Chris was the only teller on duty.

Kurt was surprised Chris was so willing to maintain eye contact with him. Like Eric Larson, Chris smiled a lot, too.

*****

The next Saturday night, after eating supper with his grandfather and washing the dishes, Kurt walked to Kensington to pay Chris a visit. Kurt arrived at his destination after dark and could see a light or two were on inside the house.

When Chris came to the door, he was wearing a white tee shirt and a pair of metal-button Levi's. His crewcut hair was a lighter brown than Kurt's, and his close-set eyes were blue.

Kurt spoke first. "I'm Kurt Reinhart. You waited on me the other day at the bank."

"Yeah, I remember."

"I thought I'd welcome you to this hopeless town. I'm surprised a guy like you would want to live here."

Chris laughed. "I like handing out cash in a bank better than serving food and cleaning tables in a dormitory dining room. This house is a nicer place to live in than a dorm room, too. More privacy, for one thing. Would you like to come in?"

*****

Kurt took a seat on the sofa in the living room.

Chris sat down on one of the two easy chairs on the other side of a coffee table Kurt's great-grandfather Otto might've fashioned from a fallen oak.

Christopher Stefanovski had grown up on an eighty-acre tenant farm in Illinois, north and west of Lafayette County. He was an only child. His mother and father were both in their late thirties when they married and he was born.

During the winter after he began college, his parents gave up farming and moved to Rockford. His father had found a job in a factory there.

Chris got by without any financial support from his parents. In his first three years at Northern, he'd not only worked in his dormitory dining room but also won scholarships with his grades and took on student loans. He asked for nothing from his parents except a place to stay during the summers, when he worked for a construction company that built inexpensive houses.

Chris hadn't decided yet what he'd do after he graduated from college.

"My major is history," he said. "I've taken enough education courses to teach in high school. Maybe that's what I'll do. I've got to pay off my loans. Then I'll go to grad school when I can afford it. I'd rather teach on the college level. And do research and write books."

"You don't look like somebody who'd do research and write books."

"What do you mean?"

"You've got an athlete's body. You play in any sports?"

"I played football in high school."

"You play for the Huskies?"

Chris shook his head. "I work out in the gym whenever I can."

Kurt looked him over again and smiled. Chris was a couple of inches taller than Kurt.

"How old are you, Kurt?"

"Sixteen."

"You're a junior at Kensington High?"

"Yeah."

"You must have a lot of friends."

Kensington was the high school for a consolidated school district that included four rural Lafayette County townships.

"No, I don't," Kurt said. "In fact, I don't have any friends."

Chris looked at Kurt as if he wondered why that would be the case.

Kurt laughed. "You're lucky. Gwendolyn likes good-looking football players. She dated one when she was in high school."

"Her husband?"

Kurt laughed. "No. Chester Smith never played football. This boyfriend was before him. He was a neighbor of my family's. My uncle says he was an attractive guy as long as he was playing football. Then he graduated from high school and spent his spare time stuffing himself with his mother's pastries. That's when Gwendolyn decided Chester might be a better choice. He was going to run his father's bank. She went to the University of Illinois the same time he did. She got a degree in English literature. He got his in accounting. Then he became the president of the bank, and she married him. They never had children."

Chris remained silent.

"I guess," Kurt said, "Gwendolyn still likes football players. Everybody around here agrees her latest coach house tenant is the best-looking boyfriend she's ever had."

Chris shook his head. "Kurt, I'm sure the people here are all good people. But maybe they talk a little too loosely. I'm not Gwendolyn Smith's boyfriend. She's not like that. Neither am I."

Kurt knew Chris would have to deny he was Gwendolyn's boyfriend, whether he was or wasn't. On the other hand, Kurt wanted to believe Chris had told him the truth.

"I'm glad I came here to see you," Kurt said, standing up. "I'll be leaving now. I have to go home. I hope I can come back and talk with you again."

Chris rose from his chair with the same smile on his face Kurt had seen at the bank.

"Please do," Chris said.

*****

The next Saturday night after supper Kurt paid another visit to the coach house.

The second bedroom in the one-story, two-bedroom house had an old wooden desk and two equally ancient wooden chairs in it but no bed.

Chris had the books he was reading piled on the desk.

On the wall above it, he'd taped a large copy of a photograph taken in September of 1957. Kurt had seen it before. It showed a white girl jeering a fifteen-year-old black girl, one of the Little Rock Nine on their way to integrate Central High School despite the presence of the Arkansas National Guard.

"Those kids and the courts," Chris said, "forced Eisenhower to act."

Eisenhower had federalized the Arkansas National Guard and sent Airborne Division troops to Little Rock to protect the Nine.

Kurt sat in the chair at the side of the desk.

Chris, in his white tee shirt and Levi's, sat in the chair facing the photo.

"Gwendolyn tells me," Chris said, "you're a straight-A kind of guy."

The schoolteachers in Gwendolyn's book club must've told her that.

"What does your grandfather say about your work in school?" Chris asked. "Does he encourage you?"

Kurt assumed Gwendolyn had provoked Chris to ask those questions.

"He doesn't say anything about it," Kurt replied.

"Does he know you've never gotten anything less than an A on your report card?"

"I assume he does," Kurt replied. "I give it to him. He looks at it. He's the one who has to sign it. A judge in Edinburgh made him my legal guardian after my mother ran off with her boyfriend and my father killed himself."

Chris winced.

"But my grandfather doesn't have to say anything," Kurt continued. "It doesn't matter. I don't care. We don't talk about things like that. I assume he expects to see nothing less than an A on my report card. Any praise would be empty."

"Gwendolyn says the teachers here talk about you. They wish all their students were so attentive."

His Grandfather's House

"And I live in a haunted house on a hill our neighbors call Mount Reinhart. I reside there with my evil, land-grabbing grandfather some people say murdered his own brother and got away with it."

"Yeah," Chris said, "I've heard that talk, too."

Kurt laughed. "I'm the man's grandson. You'd think I'd be out looking for people to murder—and just for the hell of it, too. Instead, I'm the most boring person who's ever lived."

"Are you?" Chris asked. "Gwendolyn told me an elderly neighbor of yours went insane and almost killed you and your grandfather. She said he drove his car right at you. And you were both lucky to get out of his way."

"Yeah, my grandfather tricked him into selling his farm to us. He was pissed as hell."

"Gwendolyn showed me the article and pictures in the *Edinburgh Times*. I wouldn't call what you did boring. The article said you and your grandfather ran into a burning barn to save the life of the man who'd tried to kill you."

"He was still alive when we got him out of the barn. When we put him in the neighbor's car, he had a pulse. I could feel it. He was breathing, too. He must've died on the way to the hospital. It was a damned shame. Despite what he did that day, he wasn't a bad man. He just couldn't tolerate the idea of my grandfather owning his land."

"How old were you then?"

"Thirteen, almost fourteen. It was two and a half years ago."

Chris shook his head. "You were too young to go through an attempt on your life."

"Too young? I knew what I was doing. I'd chosen to put myself where I was. I survived it without the slightest scratch on my body."

Kurt could tell Chris wasn't buying any of that.

*****

Other Saturday nights that autumn, Kurt walked to Kensington after supper.

Kurt always told his grandfather where he was going, but Henry didn't seem concerned. He merely asked Kurt to be sure he was home in time to get up for the morning chores after a good night's sleep.

"It would be difficult now," Henry said, "for Arny and me to do them without you."

"I'll never let you down," Kurt promised.

On his way to see Chris, he sometimes ran into Gwendolyn walking her sheepdog in the woods.

She would exchange greetings with Kurt, look in the direction of the house Chris lived in, turn to Kurt again and smile.

"I think he's home tonight," she'd say. "Probably waiting for you."

Chapter Twenty-Eight

During the first week in November of 1959, Arny became ill and couldn't work.

Henry was sympathetic.

"He's like his mother," he told Kurt. "He's got a bad heart. I'd rather he was in bed. If he tried to help us, he'd just be in our way."

It didn't take much to convince Kurt.

He and his grandfather, though, had many acres of corn yet to harvest. In November, they were taking a chance a snowstorm could make the remainder of the harvest a struggle and cut their yield by a greater amount than they wished to imagine.

"I'll ask Chris to help us over the weekend," Kurt said at the supper table. "He grew up on a farm. He knows all about picking corn. He's strong as a horse, too."

Henry put down his fork and looked at his grandson.

"Eric Larson told me," Kurt said, "five dollars an hour is the most guys around here get for doing part-time farmwork. I'll tell Chris we'll give him that. He'll do it. He'll use the money to pay off his car loan. That's what he wants to do right now more than anything. He had to buy the car when he took the bank job Gwendolyn offered him."

"Can you call him tonight?"

Kurt nodded his head. He'd introduced his grandfather to Chris in the bank.

"Please tell your friend," Henry said, "I'll pay him whatever you and he think is fair."

*****

Henry, Kurt and Chris worked well past sunset on Saturday as well as Sunday.

Kurt had correctly guessed Chris was like his grandfather, Eric Larson and himself. They went at hard physical work as if they enjoyed it. Kurt couldn't explain why they did that, but the result was the same in all four cases. The work got done.

Veterans Day was on Wednesday of the next week, the bank was closed, and Chris had no classes to attend. He helped Kurt and his grandfather again that day. By the time they finished their work, long after sunset, the corn harvest on Henry Reinhart's farm was accomplished.

While Kurt prepared a late supper, his grandfather and Chris sat on the steps outside the kitchen door talking.

Kurt heard his grandfather ask the history student if he thought the Battle of Stalingrad was the turning point in the Second World War. Reverend Crosley had long insisted, from his pulpit, it wasn't. D-day, according to him, was.

"Stalingrad is the story liberal, pinko eggheads in this country would have us believe!" Cecil liked to thunder. "The story God tells me takes place on the beaches of Normandy!"

Chris laughed and said he'd have to agree with the liberal, pinko eggheads.

*****

When the cold, ice and snow of winter came that year, Kurt continued to see Chris on Saturday evenings. But now Chris picked Kurt up and brought him home in his red-and-white 1954 Chevy.

Elaine and Arny reprised the roles they'd played in Lorelei's affair, as observers behind parted curtains. Other Kensingtonians took notice using similar means.

So the Reverend Cecil Crosley learned that the sixteen-year-old grandson of Henry Reinhart and a twenty-one-year-old college student he referred to as a "leftist" spent their Saturday evenings together in Gwendolyn Smith's coach house in the woods.

Cecil soon included in his sermons his understanding of what an infamous crime against nature was.

"It often involves a clever and still youthful man using his superficial physical appeal to get what he wants," Cecil said. "Using it to lure a foolish boy who's never bothered himself to learn right from wrong. To lure that wayward boy into the man's depraved and wholly unnatural world where men lust after men."

The first time Cecil included that indictment in his sermon, Gwendolyn and Chester Smith walked out of his church in the middle of it.

"Just like your nephew did at his grandma's funeral," somebody in Kensington told Elaine, who repeated the information for Kurt and

Arny.

Cecil soon learned he'd deprived himself of the Smiths' generous additions to the cash on his collection plates not just for one Sunday but for good. The Smiths had joined the Episcopalian church in Edinburgh.

That only led Cecil to include a "money changer and his wife" in his denunciation. They, after all, provided "the house where the infamous crime against nature takes place!"

Many in Cecil's own flock dismissed those stories.

"Cecil will say anything," the owner of the bakery in Kensington told Arny, "to smear your father."

During their Saturday nights together, Kurt and Chris mostly talked, and a lot of that was about the books they were reading. They'd sometimes watch a program on the furnished television in the living room—but usually only to make comments on what little interest it had for them.

Lately also, they'd often let a game of chess or two—Chris was teaching Kurt how to play it—interrupt their witty remarks before it was time for Chris to take Kurt home.

And return him to his grandfather's house untouched.

*****

In the spring of 1960, the boys who planned to play football for Kensington High in the fall asked Chris and Kurt to skirmish with them. They knew Chris had quarterbacked his team to state championships in his junior and senior years in high school.

Kurt played any position they wanted him to play. Despite his lack of practice, he could often find a stratagem—sometimes only a slight move of his body one way or the other—to confound his opponents. And because he wasn't seeking a position on the team, it was easy for him to let an unskilled adversary prevail once in a while and not suffer undue humiliation.

"Good catch!" he'd shout to a receiver who'd caught a touchdown pass Kurt knew he could've deflected or intercepted.

The players on the football team agreed the Reverend Crosley's vicious insinuations regarding Chris and Kurt were a joke. Athletes as good as they were couldn't be "queer." It was ridiculous to think they'd want to have sex with each other.

The team members had taken showers with Kurt and Chris. Neither, they said, had shown the slightest interest in doing anything with another guy.

It was obvious they were friends. But so what? They liked to talk about history and all the other serious stuff somebody had to think about.

"Let it be them," they said, laughing.

*****

"I wish I could've found a friend like Chris when I was your age."

So Arny informed Kurt one evening when they were feeding the cattle and hogs by themselves. Henry was still out in the field on a tractor planting oats.

Kurt emptied his pails and looked at his uncle.

"But you'd better be careful," Arny said. "You know what Cecil's saying."

"I know what he's saying," Kurt said. "And he's full of shit. Chris and I haven't done a goddamned thing. We're just friends."

"That's what I tell people," Arny said.

"I only wish," Kurt said, "what that asshole is saying was true."

Arny gave his nephew a faraway look. "I can imagine you would."

*****

Arny wasn't feeling well again when the time came to plant corn.

Henry and Kurt agreed. Arny had suffered enough. They went to his bedside together and told him not to worry for a moment.

His illness gave them an excuse to hire Chris to help them another weekend, and the next weekend as well.

During the last of the corn-planting suppers Chris ate with them, he explained why he thought the persons who ran things in America and Russia were sending rockets into space. They'd both have their people believe the prize was to be the first, as in a game, to land a spaceship on the moon with humans aboard. But they more specifically wanted to demonstrate to their counterparts on the other side how advanced they were in launching intercontinental ballistic missiles capable of precisely landing nuclear bombs on the other's military installations and cities. Each side wanted the other deeply afraid.

Henry nodded his head. "That makes damned good sense to me."

Kurt looked at Chris and smirked.

When Chris had previously tried out the theory on him, Kurt predicted his grandfather would enjoy its unvarnished realism.

Chapter Twenty-Nine

Monday, May 16, 1960, the day following the weekend Chris had helped Kurt and Henry finish their planting, was Kurt's seventeenth birthday. After supper at Elaine and Arny's that evening, Kurt declined their invitation to watch television with them.

He left their house with his grandfather, said good-by to him, and walked to Kensington.

Kurt did what he'd done the first time he'd visited Chris the previous September. He sat down on the couch in the living room.

And Chris, surprised to see Kurt, did as he'd done that other evening. He took a seat on the chair directly across the coffee table from his visitor.

"I've got a question for you," Kurt said.

Chris sighed. "I know."

"Have you decided what you're going to do?"

"I've made a decision."

"I hope you've decided to take the teaching assistant position they offered you at Northern. I also hope you've decided to stay here and continue working part-time at the bank."

Chris shook his head. "If I did that, I wouldn't have enough money to pay my bills. I'd have to borrow more money and go deeper in debt than I already am. I've gone over the figures a dozen times. I've turned down the teaching assistant position. I did it today."

Kurt felt as if he'd taken a punch in his gut.

He'd offered to ask his grandfather to loan Chris the money he needed to continue his education. Chris had begged him not to do that. Chris said it didn't matter who loaned him the money. He'd still have to pay it back with interest.

"So what are you going to do?" Kurt asked, unable to hide the fear in his voice.

"The high school I went to offered me a job. They called me this morning. I accepted it. I'll teach history and help the coach with the PE classes. They'll pay me extra to handle summer school. I'll teach anything kids have flunked and need to take over."

"Starting this summer?"

"Starting this summer."

"Where will you live?"

"With my mom and dad in Rockford. I'll commute."

"You're giving up on getting a higher degree?"

"I'm not giving up on it. I'm just postponing it until after I've paid down my student loans."

Kurt shook his head. "This is the worst news I've ever heard."

"Why do you say that, Kurt?"

"You won't have any time for me in your life."

Chris sighed again. "Maybe that'll be best for both of us."

That felt to Kurt like an even more powerful blow to his belly.

"You mean," he asked, "it'll be best for two men who lust after men?"

Chris made no attempt to respond to that question.

"You mean," Kurt asked, "for two guys who've spent every Saturday night together for the last nine months?"

Again, Chris remained silent.

"Wouldn't you agree," Kurt asked, "two guys like that have to be, as my uncle would say, homosexual? Or, as most people would put it, queer?"

Chris grimaced. "I'd much rather we called ourselves gay."

Now Kurt was speechless.

"And we're men," Chris said, "who lust after men. The minister is right about that."

Kurt found his voice. "I'm glad to hear you say that. Now we can get right to the point. I'm in love with you. And I'm damned sure you're in love with me."

Having won a battle, Chris chose to retreat and remain silent again.

"Goddamnit," Kurt said, "I want you and me to be boyfriends."

"We are friends, Kurt. I think that's obvious."

"Do you love me?"

Chris thought a bit before he attempted to answer that question.

"I love my mother and father," he said. "I'd have to say I love you, too."

"Come on," Kurt said. "Do you love me the way you'd love a boyfriend? Are we gay boyfriends, or aren't we? Answer me that."

"You're still in high school, Kurt. Gay boyfriends usually have sex with one another. I told you—I believe it was the second time you came to see me here last September—I'll never have sex with anybody who's still in high school. I won't do that."

"I know you won't, and I respect you for it. But I'm not asking you to have sex with me."

Kurt looked Chris up and down as if his host had removed his clothes and were sitting in front of him naked.

"I can still beat off thinking about you," Kurt said. "I do it every day, and I'm not about to stop now."

Kurt could tell Chris was making every effort not to reveal whether that mattered to him.

Chris shook his head. "I don't think we should consider ourselves boyfriends, Kurt. I think you're too young to be making that kind of decision."

"Too young? Do you know how old I am?"

"I know how old you are. You turned seventeen today. That's why I wasn't expecting to see you. I'd assumed you'd want to spend your birthday with your family."

"How did you know this is my birthday? I never told you the sixteenth of May is my birthday."

"Yes, you did. When you took me to see your family's graveyard, you did. You told me the date of your father's death on his headstone, May 17, 1947, was the day after your fourth birthday. I like math as much as you do."

"You remembered that?"

"I did."

"And even at seventeen, I'm too young to decide who I want for a boyfriend?"

"Especially at seventeen."

"When do you think I'll be old enough to do that?"

"Maybe a year from now. When you're eighteen, and you've finished high school."

"So I have to wait a whole year to find out whether you and I can be boyfriends?"

"I don't think you should wait for anything, Kurt. I think you should feel free to become friends with other guys, especially other guys your own age."

"I don't want other guys to be my boyfriend."

Kurt knew he was getting loud.

"I want you, Chris," he said. "I'm in love with you. I want you to be my boyfriend."

"People have been known to change their minds about things

like that."

"I'll never change my mind about you."

Chris shook his head again. "Please don't talk that way, Kurt. You could meet somebody you'd rather have for a boyfriend than me."

"That isn't going to happen."

When Kurt concluded those remarks, he saw something he hadn't previously seen.

Chris had tears in his eyes. He was using the lower end of his tee shirt to wipe them away.

"I'm sorry, Kurt. I really am. I feel as if the last nine months I've been living in a dream with you. But I think it's time we brought it to an end, at least for a while."

"For a year, you mean?"

"I'm afraid so. That's why your talk about our being boyfriends doesn't make any sense. I'm going to be a high school teacher. You don't attend the high school where I'll be teaching, but you'll be a high school student for another year. I don't think we should be seeing each other during that time. It wouldn't be right. A high school teacher and a high school student shouldn't be boyfriends."

"Even if they're not having sex?"

"Yeah, even if they're not having sex—but they both want to."

Kurt stared at Chris, who was using his tee shirt to dry his eyes again.

"You admit," Kurt asked, "you want to have sex with me?"

"You know I do."

"And simply because we want to have sex with each other, we can't see each other for another year?"

Chris shrugged his shoulders.

"I'll be damned," Kurt said. "My seventeenth birthday turned out to be the worst fucking day of my life."

"I'm sorry," Chris said. "I really am. But I don't see what else I can do."

In the momentary pause following that exchange, they could hear thunder rumbling in the distance.

"You're right about one thing," Kurt said. "I'm not waiting around another year for you. If you can't tell me we're boyfriends right now, and if we can't see each other for another year, that's the end of it. You don't love me the way I love you, and you never will. I'll have to find some way to forget about you."

Kurt, who had tears of his own running down his face, stood up. "I'm leaving," he said.

Chris remained in his chair, still wiping his eyes.

"Let me put my shoes on," he said. "I'll give you a ride home."

"I'm walking home," Kurt said. "I don't want to be seen with you again. I don't want people thinking we're boyfriends—because we're not."

*****

The third thunderstorm of the day arrived when Kurt reached the road Albert Rauenthaler and Edna and Karl Boecker used to live on, the road that was now the northern border of Henry Reinhart's farm.

By the time Kurt ran up the hill to his grandfather's house, slipping more than once to his hands and knees in the May mud, he was as frightened by the lightning as he was soaked by the rain.

He was glad, though, he'd learned how weak the man of his dreams was.

Kurt was certain he could find somebody more daring than Chris Stefanovski to spend his life with.

Chapter Thirty

An hour after supper the next Saturday night, Kurt's grandfather asked him if Chris was coming to pick him up. "No," Kurt replied.

Henry looked at Kurt across the dining room table as if he shared his loss.

Arny had tried to warn his father as early as Wednesday that something had happened between Kurt and Chris.

But Henry had seen fit to lash out at the messenger.

"I've never understood why you listen to gossip like that," he said. "If you choose to do it, if you can't resist it, all I ask you is, don't try to pass it on to me. I don't want to hear it."

Arny didn't have the heart to tell his father this news wasn't gossip—it had come from Kurt himself.

But now Henry saw it was true. Something had happened.

Grandson and grandfather bore their disappointment together that night and chose not to speak of it again.

*****

On May 30, 1960, Memorial Day, Gwendolyn Smith called Kurt.

Chris had moved out of the coach house after taking his last exam at Northern. He'd decided not to stay for the graduation ceremony. He would receive his diploma in the mail.

Kurt had left some books in the coach house. Chris had asked Gwendolyn if she'd make sure he got them back.

Kurt drove his grandfather's car, now a 1958 Pontiac, to pick up the books that evening.

When Gwendolyn came to the door, she took off her glasses and let them hang from her neck on a silver chain.

"The books are on his desk," she said, as if Chris still lived in the house. "He wanted me to tell you he finished reading them all. He's grateful you loaned them to him."

Kurt forced himself to smile. He felt more like crying.

"He told me," Gwendolyn continued, "you and he had a falling out. That's all he said. The details are none of my business, but I have to be honest with you. Whatever caused the dispute between you and him, I think it's a shame. You seemed so good for one another."

For a school year, Kurt and Chris each had one close friend in the world—the other. Gwendolyn had probably guessed that.

"I suppose you know," she said, "he's moved back to his parents' house in Rockford. And he's taken a job teaching history and PE at the high school in his hometown."

"He told me," Kurt replied, "that's what he intended to do."

"To be honest, I don't understand why he didn't take that teaching assistant position they offered him at Northern instead. He could've continued living in this house and working part-time at the bank. I would've gotten his pay at the bank increased. Our customers liked him a lot. I believe he should've continued his education. I think he could do much better than teaching history and PE in a high school."

Gwendolyn looked closely at Kurt when they reached the room with the desk.

"But maybe I'm wrong," she said. "Maybe it's for the best he decided to live with his mom and dad again. He called me this afternoon. They found out his mother has cancer, and it's the terminal kind. Chris will be a comfort to her."

When Kurt and Gwendolyn carried his books to the car, they both had tears in their eyes.

*****

Kurt and Arny were doing the evening chores by themselves again. Henry was in the toolshed sharpening the mower blades on his emery wheel. As soon as the dew dried the next morning, Kurt would begin cutting the hay.

"You must've fallen in love with Chris," Arny said.

Kurt finished filling his five-gallon pails with ground corn and looked at his uncle.

"I did," he said. "I should've known it wouldn't work out, but I did it anyway."

"And you never did anything with him?" Arny asked. "Not even once?"

"Not even once."

"I hope you can get him back. I see why you fell for him. If a guy like that had ever come into my life before I married Elaine, I would've done what you did. I would've fallen in love with him."

His Grandfather's House

"I don't think Chris and I will get back together," Kurt said. "He was my best friend during my junior year in high school. I'm grateful for that. But I think it's hopeless for me to expect more."

*****

In the summer that followed, it didn't matter how many days Arny was unable or unwilling to help with the work. Elaine only needed to make his unavailability known to Henry or Kurt, and they accepted without question whatever reason she gave them.

All Kurt wanted to do was work. He was out to prove to himself he could get by without Chris. For one thing, he had his grandfather's farm to think about and take care of. He also had an ailing uncle to fill in for.

*****

In the first months of his first job out of college, Chris found himself in trouble. That summer, the Democrats nominated John Kennedy for president and the Republicans, Richard Nixon. And even though his hometown was as staunchly Republican as Kensington, Chris had volunteered to work for Kennedy.

When that became known, some of the citizens in the school district demanded to know why such a radical should be allowed to teach history in their high school. Since Chris didn't have tenure, his opponents insisted the school board fire him immediately—before he "poisoned the well," as they put it, of their children's minds.

Kennedy's people alerted the media in Chicago and throughout the state. A school board in a traditionally Republican northern Illinois town would meet to consider firing a teacher for nothing more than working for Kennedy's election on his own time.

The media took note. Photographs of Chris appeared on the front pages of the Chicago papers. The Chicago television stations interviewed him for their evening news programs.

Kurt felt the full extent of his loss when he saw the photo of Chris on the front page of his grandfather's *Tribune* and watched him on the newscasts with Arny and Elaine.

There was the beautiful, thoughtful and kind man who was no

longer a part of his life.

The American Civil Liberties Union in Chicago offered Chris free legal representation before the school board and in any lawsuit he might wish to file if he lost his job. For the ACLU, it was a straightforward question of free speech.

And, Kurt imagined, the good looks of their honest-but-poor client toiling in the backwoods as a schoolteacher didn't hurt the publicity value of his case.

*****

But Chris's hometown was also less than five years past the two glorious seasons in which he'd led their football team to state championships. A number of people began to wonder what the fuss was all about. At his worst, Chris was only a Democrat.

The school board held its meeting in the high school gym to accommodate the crowd and the media people. The many students and teachers who were partial to Chris filled the rows of folding chairs on the gym floor. Most of his former teammates were there as well. Chris, his lawyers and the persons chosen to speak for him sat in the front row. The reporters and camera people stood on either side of them. Townspeople packed the bleachers.

The board first heard those in favor of dismissing Chris. They all tried, at length, to make two things clear. Their community had no need of "a liberal, leftist agitator" in its high school faculty. And the volunteer work Chris was doing for Kennedy had nothing to do with the matter.

The lead lawyer for Chris invoked the First Amendment in a brief but passionate statement setting forth the right of public-school teachers to engage in political activities on their own time.

The last student who spoke up for Chris was the daughter of a nurse who was caring for his mother. She pointed out that removing Chris from his position would woefully burden his family. Chris and his father were paying out of pocket for much of his mother's care. They'd both given her their solemn promise she'd never spend a day in a nursing home.

After that student, wiping her eyes, sat down, the gym was quiet. When the time came for Chris to speak, he gazed at the cameras as if he couldn't understand why they were aimed at him. It took him less than thirty seconds to say his lawyer and the others who'd spoken on his behalf had made every argument that needed to be made for him to keep his job.

The president of the board asked the other members if any of them wished to make a motion to dismiss Mr. Stefanovski.

The members, staring at Chris, chose to remain silent.

"Hearing no motion," the president said, "the board has concluded its consideration of the petition to dismiss Christopher Stefanovski. Petition denied."

She began the victory celebration herself. She called what she said would be "a brief recess," walked to where Chris sat, took his hand, pulled him to his feet, and gave him a hug.

The students, teachers and former teammates on the gym floor rose to their feet and cheered.

Chapter Thirty-One

Later that evening, Kurt was in Elaine and Arny's living room for their favorite ten o'clock newscast from Chicago.

"A high school history teacher working for Kennedy keeps his job," the announcer began the story.

Kurt had other opportunities to see Chris on television that autumn. Chris spent his weekends on college campuses in Illinois. He appeared at events and gave inspiring speeches for Kennedy. He never failed to emphasize the senator's heroics in the Second World War.

When Chris spoke at Northern in DeKalb, Kurt knew the Chicago stations would be there. So he sat watching once again with Elaine and Arny.

Chris had moved on to his next adventure after his conquest of Mount Reinhart. It was obvious he didn't need Kurt.

Kurt hoped Chris would find, or had already found, some man worthy enough to be his partner. Kurt had to admit he'd destroyed his own chance to become that person.

*****

When election day arrived, Elaine, Arny and Henry drove to the Kensington town hall together. When they got there, Elaine announced to the Republican officials they'd be casting three votes for Kennedy.

Neither Henry nor Arny attempted to contradict her. And silence, of course, could only mean guilt.

*****

That evening, Kurt showed up with a bottle of beer to watch the late returns with Elaine and Arny. Males in Illinois couldn't drink alcohol legally until they were twenty-one. As in his father's day, though, his classmates were drinking in bars and at parties—and not always limiting themselves, as Kurt did, to a single beer in an evening.

If the Democrats won in Illinois, Kurt hoped he might glimpse Chris at the victory celebration in Chicago.

Arny looked at Kurt. "You seem to miss him an awful lot."

Kurt shook his head. "I can get by perfectly okay without him."

"But you'd like to get him back," Arny said. "If I were you, I'd want to get him back."

Kurt hadn't imagined his uncle would discuss Chris in such a manner in front of Elaine.

"I won't deny that," Kurt said.

Elaine looked at her husband and nephew and sighed.

"I can't say," she said, "you two don't have good taste."

Arny scoffed. "I don't know if I've got good taste, but at least I'm not completely dead. I do know a good-looking man when I see one."

"Eric Larson?" Kurt asked.

"Yeah," Arny replied. "Absolutely."

"Absolutely," Elaine agreed, with another sigh.

*****

That was also the night Elaine and Arny told Kurt they wanted to live in Florida after they retired from their work on the farm.

Kurt had seen the colorful brochures for ocean lots lying around their house.

"We're sick and tired of the winters here," Arny said.

"You can come and visit us," Elaine added.

Kurt, who hadn't gone farther from his grandfather's farm than the Chicago lakefront one day with Chris, couldn't imagine taking a trip to Florida. His grandfather could no longer do the chores by himself. If Arny wasn't available to help, Kurt would have to stay home. Long-distance traveling wouldn't be possible for him. What was Elaine thinking?

Lately, though, Kurt had noticed, some of his aunt's remarks were strange.

What was her purpose, he'd wondered, in talking about voting for Kennedy in front of the election officials? She had to know she'd only anger the Republicans like Chester Smith who ran things in Kensington and Lafayette County. On the other hand, Kurt had to admit, who was he to blame her for amusing herself at their expense?

*****

Kennedy carried Illinois and its twenty-seven electoral votes by a narrow margin.

His Grandfather's House

Kurt soon wished the campaigning hadn't come to an end.

No further opportunity arose for him to see Chris on television.

And what was Chris up to now?

He could've written or called Kurt, but he hadn't.

Kurt likewise could've written or called Chris, but he hadn't.

*****

One of Kurt's classmates, Rodney Adenauer, took it upon himself that autumn to replace Chris as Kurt's best friend. During their younger years, Rodney had often kept himself close to Kurt on the playground and in the gym. Kurt knew Rodney was seeking his protection from the bigger and stronger boys who liked to pick on him.

In their senior year in high school, Rodney and Kurt began eating lunch together, just the two of them. Rodney was still a few inches shorter than Kurt, but he'd become brawny enough to defend himself if he had to.

Rodney was an only child. His mother and father, tenant farmers on a hundred-acre hog farm, had adopted him when they were in their late forties. They'd tried and failed to have children of their own. People said they went to an orphanage in Chicago and picked out Rodney because he was the cutest child available. Some people speculated that he had dark brown hair and eyes because his real parents were Italian or Greek.

One day, Rodney told Kurt he was gay. Kurt wasn't surprised to learn that, but he hadn't anticipated Rodney being so open about it.

"I assume," Rodney said, "you are, too."

"Of course, I'm gay," Kurt said. "And I'm glad to know you are. Thank you for being so blunt about it."

Kurt looked around at the other students and teachers in the lunchroom and shrugged.

"But I don't think it'll do us any good to tell anybody else," he said.

"Yeah," Rodney agreed. "Let 'em wonder all they want. We'll keep 'em guessing."

He turned back to Kurt.

"So can we talk to one another now," he asked, "the way gay guys do?"

Kurt laughed. "We can at least try to imagine how they do it."

*****

During their next lunch hour, Rodney started asking the questions Kurt had assumed were coming.

"Is Chris gay?"

That was the first.

"Yeah," Kurt replied.

Rodney took a deep breath. "A gay man who looks like that. Wow."

Kurt had expected his answer would please Rodney.

"Were you in love with him?" Rodney asked.

That was the second question.

"Of course," Kurt replied. "Deeply. Insanely."

"Were you doing it with him?"

That was the third, but Kurt could tell it was the most important one of them all.

"No," Kurt replied without hesitation. "Chris and I never had sex."

"Really? That's kinda disappointing."

Rodney could sometimes say the most irritating things.

"I assumed you were doing it with Chris," he continued. "Lucky you, I thought."

Kurt looked at his self-appointed friend, who fed hogs morning and night, and, like Kurt himself in his boots, shoveled manure off the floor of the barn where it fell and spread it on the fields where it could do some good.

"I would've loved having sex with Chris," Kurt said. "As soon as we met, though, he told me he'd never have sex with anybody still young enough to be in high school. He had strong feelings on that subject."

Rodney couldn't conceal how interested he was in what Kurt was telling him.

"Why did you and Chris break up?" he asked. "Why don't you still see him?"

As if he were Elaine, Kurt sighed. "It was his idea. He was going to be a high school teacher. He couldn't be seeing a boyfriend who was a high school student, even if we weren't having sex. I blew up and told him I never wanted to see him again. That was the biggest mistake I ever made. It was the day I turned seventeen, the worst damned day of my life."

Rodney laid his fork down and put his hand on Kurt's shoulder.

"I'm sorry, Kurt," he said. "What a shame. You and Chris seemed to have everything. Looks. Brains. Everything."

"And it didn't matter, did it? We don't have anything now."

Chapter Thirty-Two

On Christmas Day in 1960, Kurt ate his evening meal with Elaine and Arny in their house. Elaine had roasted a ham with sweet potatoes from Kurt's garden.

Elaine and Arny no longer decorated their house for any holiday, not even Christmas.

Henry had told Kurt they'd finally come to their senses on that subject.

Henry didn't come down to Elaine and Arny's house for their holiday dinner. He seemed to be suffering a cold or the flu and went straight to bed after the evening chores.

"I thought he looked terrible," Arny said to Kurt. "He should've let you and me do everything today."

"He's seventy-two going on seventy-three," Elaine said. "He isn't going to live forever."

Kurt glared at his aunt.

"Have you thought about that?" she asked him, returning his look. "Have you thought about what happens to us when that old man up there dies?"

Kurt tried not to show Elaine how much her question had disturbed him.

"It hadn't crossed my mind," he replied.

"I didn't think so," Elaine said. "Your boyfriends keep you too busy for that."

"I don't have a boyfriend," Kurt said. "I've never had one."

Neither Elaine nor Arny chose to dispute the veracity of those remarks.

"We'll have to decide what to do with the farm," Arny said.

Too bad, Kurt thought, his grandfather wasn't a god who could live forever and protect his all-too-human grandson from this.

"You and Arny will inherit it," Elaine said. "The two of you will have to decide what to do with it."

Kurt could see a Florida brochure lying open on the counter beneath the china cabinet behind Elaine.

"Elaine and I," Arny said, "would like to sell the farm. We'd take our half of the proceeds and move down to Florida. No more frigid northern winters for us."

Kurt felt as if he were sharing a meal with two strangers.

"Sell his farm?" Kurt asked. "The farm he spent his life putting together?"

"The farm he put together," Elaine said, "using every trick in the book, murder included."

"He never murdered anybody," Kurt said, his voice louder than he'd intended it to be. "He never broke a single law putting his farm together. People have made a lot of accusations against him, but nobody's ever proved a goddamned thing."

Elaine scoffed. "Aren't we granddaddy's loyal grandson this merry Christmas Day?"

"Whatever the fuck I am," Kurt said, "I'll never agree to sell his farm."

Elaine looked at Arny without attempting to hide her annoyance. "I told you," she said, "that's what he'd say."

*****

"It's supposed to be a deep, dark secret," Rodney said. "So please don't repeat any of this to anybody."

"You can count on me," Kurt said. "I've learned how to keep secrets."

Rodney laughed. He and Kurt both brought lunches to school they put together at home. They enjoyed their independence from the people they lived with, even as they toiled outside school hours to keep them alive and well. They also freely sampled the items on the other's tray.

"A few years ago," Rodney said, "I found the key to the box my legal parents keep their important documents in. I read my adoption papers. My real mother is my legal mother's niece."

Kurt looked at Rodney. They both had mothers who'd abandoned them?

"Does she acknowledge you as her son?" Kurt asked.

"Oh, no. She had me out of wedlock. She stayed in a home in Indiana when she was pregnant with me. She's friendly to me at family gatherings, but she doesn't want anybody to find out I'm her son. She lives in Edinburgh with her husband and their four children. Those kids don't know they're my half sisters and half brothers. Her husband doesn't know either."

Kurt had seen the woman Rodney said was his real mother. She had dark brown hair and eyes.

Rodney took an apple slice from Kurt's tray, dipped it in Kurt's honey and raisins, and lifted it to his mouth.

"Want to know who my father was?" Rodney asked. "And why I'm so good-looking?"

Kurt laughed.

"You'll never guess," Rodney said.

"I agree," Kurt said. "I'll never guess."

"He was Eric Larson's older brother."

Kurt left his fork on his tray and looked at Rodney. "The one who got killed in the war?"

"He's the one. But not until after he knocked up my mother and refused to marry her. He signed the adoption papers and joined the army instead. It must've been about the same time your dad did. But my father never got his ass out of Italy. He's buried over there. Near where he died, Eric told me."

More brown hair and eyes from the Larsons, Kurt thought.

"Does Eric know he's your uncle?" he asked.

Rodney shook his head. "Nobody in the Larson family knows I'm related to them."

"What a shame."

"Now my legal mom and dad want me to find some nice young lady to have kids with."

"But you're only seventeen."

"They say I'm not too young to start looking. They'd die if they knew I was gay. They'd have to give up all hope. They tell me only grandkids can fix what ails them."

*****

Kurt stayed home from school and viewed Kennedy's inauguration with Elaine and Arny.

Kurt liked the speech, but his aunt and uncle chose to wax cynical.

"Your dad," Elaine said to Kurt, "asked what he could do for his country."

Arny scoffed. "And see what that got Johnny. A hole up there on the hill."

Kurt wished he could've watched the ceremony with Chris.

"We saw a lawyer," Elaine said. "He told us Arny can force you to sell the farm."

So on Friday, January 20, 1961, Elaine and Arny gave Kurt their ultimatum.

"When your grandfather dies," Arny said, "we'll sell the farm and split the proceeds and the bank accounts down the middle with you."

"We'll all be wealthy," Elaine said, turning to Kurt. "You might find yourself a man you'll like even more than you did Chris. You'll have all the money you'll ever need. Who could ask for more?"

Kurt could. He could ask for his grandfather and Chris.

He shook his head. "Why are you two talking so much about what might happen many, many years down the road? The person who owns this farm is still alive and well. You can't force him to sell his farm. I don't need to see a goddamned lawyer to tell me that."

"You don't want to imagine your granddad gone from your world," Elaine said.

"No, I don't," Kurt said. "I need him in my world. It wouldn't be complete without him."

*****

Rodney was blunt. "What are you going to do now? Find yourself a new boyfriend?"

Those questions surprised Kurt as much as Elaine and Arny's threats had.

"I'll have to," he said. "Eventually."

"Eventually?" Rodney asked. "Why not now?"

"Why are you asking?"

"I could be your boyfriend. I'd love to have sex with you."

When Kurt refused to blink, Rodney felt free to up the ante.

"I could meet you after supper tonight," he said. "Your barn or mine?"

Kurt realized he was no longer a boy. He'd have to try harder to be an adult.

"Thank you for your invitation," he said. "I take it you're serious. I do like you. And I'll seriously consider what you're offering me."

"But you won't say yes right now?"

"No, I won't."

"You're still in love with Chris?"

"Yeah, I am. I admit it. Somehow, I've got to get over him."

Rodney shook his head. "I don't understand. If you're still in love with Chris, why do you have to get over him?"

"Because I'll never be the person he deserves to have at his side, to live with. I know what's wrong with me. I'm like my grandfather and father. I'm like everybody in my family. My mother and my aunt, too. We want what we want, and we'll do whatever it takes to get it. We don't really care what we're doing to the people who happen to be in our way."

Rodney looked at Kurt and shook his head again. "You're not like that."

"Don't you see what I did with Chris? I insisted he tell me he was my boyfriend. He couldn't do that and be a high school teacher. But I didn't give a damn."

Rodney had paused eating his lunch.

"You're kinda hard on yourself," he said.

"I should be. I was only thinking about myself. And then I told him I wanted nothing more to do with him. I must've been insane. That's what people say about the Reinharts. We're all insane. Chris knows he's better off without me. I'll never get a second chance with him."

Chapter Thirty-Three

"You know what?" Rodney asked Kurt the next day at lunch.

"What?"

"Even with all your faults, you could still be my boyfriend."

Kurt looked at Rodney. He wanted to say yes, go someplace where they could be alone, kiss him on his lips, and get it over with.

Still, Rodney wasn't Chris. Not yet at least.

*****

Rodney moaned. Kurt's rejection had left him with no other prospective boyfriend in the area. He'd have to take the train into Chicago and walk the streets until he met someone. He'd be forced to get by on his youth and looks alone.

"Don't get me wrong," he said. "I'm not asking for sympathy. I know I can do it."

Kurt laughed and cut a corner off Rodney's chicken salad sandwich with his knife and fork. Rodney had baked the bread.

"There's at least one other gay guy out here in the sticks," Kurt said. "He lives just north of Edinburgh. He's the same age we are. I'd imagine you'd like him, too. He's my cousin."

Tim Juergen lived on a 240-acre hog farm with his parents and three brothers, one older than him and two younger. They were tenant farmers.

Kurt had met Tim the previous February when the Juergens held their annual reunion. It was always on the Sunday nearest the birthday of the oldest member of the family, and at her house and expense— excepting, of course, the "dishes to pass" the guests brought.

Aunt Juergen, as they called her, had never married. She'd used her inheritance as the only child of tenant farmers to pay one-quarter of the purchase price of a 160-acre farm. She'd talked the president of the bank in Edinburgh into loaning her the money to pay the other three-quarters. He'd told her it would be the first time the bank had made such a loan to a "spinster."

Aunt Juergen worked the farm with a woman whose name she'd put on the deed as a joint owner with the right of survivorship. Sometimes bidding at auctions against Henry Reinhart, they bought calves shipped in from "out west" to fatten on corn and alfalfa and sell in Chicago. Having no children to raise, they paid off Aunt Juergen's mortgage loan long before it was due. When they decided to retire from doing the farmwork themselves, they built a tenant house and rented their farm to Eric Larson's parents.

After her friend died, Aunt Juergen was once again the sole owner of her farm. She told her relatives she had a will, but she wouldn't say who was in it and who wasn't.

One Saturday evening in Edinburgh, she saw Kurt and Chris. They'd come to see *Suddenly, Last Summer* at the Palace. She thought Kurt looked like a nearly grown-up version of a thirteen-year-old boy she'd seen in a photo on the front page of the *Edinburgh Times* a few years back.

At the time it appeared, she showed the picture to others in the Juergen family. They agreed the boy an enraged neighbor had almost killed, Henry Reinhart's grandson, had to be the child Lorelei had given birth to before she ran off to California with her lawyer boyfriend. The solemn but heroic boy in the photo on the front page of the newspaper was a Juergen.

Aunt Juergen introduced herself to Kurt and Chris. They viewed the film together. She invited Kurt to the next Juergen reunion at her house. He could, of course, bring a guest.

Kurt took Chris. After Tim met them, he remained at their side until the party was over.

"He's gay," Kurt told Rodney. "No straight guy would've done that."

*****

Rodney was Kurt's guest at the Juergen family gathering in February of 1961. As soon as Tim saw them, he came at them like a bee starving for nectar.

At first, Aunt Juergen glared at Rodney as if he were an impostor. After a while, though, she smiled at him, and he went over to her for a chat.

Kurt turned to Tim. With their light-brown hair and eyes, broad shoulders and narrow hips, they could've passed for brothers.

"I'm gay," Kurt said.

Tim, who wasn't ready for that remark, managed a wan smile nevertheless.

"So is Chris," Kurt said, marching on like a soldier. "So is Rodney."

Kurt looked his cousin in the eye.

"So what are you?" he asked. "Gay? Straight? You don't know what the fuck you are?"

Tim drew himself as close to Kurt as his observing relatives would allow.

"I'm with you," he whispered in Kurt's ear. "I like guys."

*****

Kurt told Tim what he'd told Rodney. He was still in love with Chris.

Tim and Rodney became boyfriends the next evening—in Rodney's parents' car on a dark, wooded side of an infrequently traveled road.

Kurt was jealous as hell they'd both beat him to it. And after that, he had to listen at lunch almost every day while Rodney went on about how wonderful Tim was.

But Kurt knew any objection from him would only emphasize what a damned fool he was. The chump who'd lost Chris. The clown who'd deserved to lose Chris.

*****

Within a few weeks of the first night of their late-winter euphoria, Rodney and Tim chose the same evening after school to inform their families they were in love.

Their parents, and Tim's brothers, responded as Kurt had expected they would. If Rodney and Tim were truly homosexual, they were no longer welcome in their families.

Both sets of parents also claimed they'd seen this coming. Henry Reinhart's grandson—the one who'd told a Christian minister his sermons were bullshit, the one who'd almost gotten himself killed in his grandfather's feud with his neighbor—was obviously behind it.

Rodney's parents knew they couldn't survive on their farm without Rodney's help. They therefore decided to give up their lease and quit farming. They found jobs on the custodial staff at the new farm implement factory in Edinburgh. They bought a house in a new subdivision that featured inexpensive, prefabricated dwellings. They told Rodney he'd have to live elsewhere.

Tim's parents also told him to get out of their house—and to stay away from his younger brothers.

*****

Eric Larson's father suffered a heart attack and died. Eric's mother decided to move in with Eric and his wife to help take care of their five children, all of them born within the first five years of their marriage.

Aunt Juergen's tenant house would soon be empty. Tim and Rodney went to see her.

She called the neighbors who'd exchanged work with their families. All of them agreed, she said, Tim and Rodney were good, strong boys who were always ready and willing to put in long hours no matter what the job was, even in the worst heat and humidity of the summer.

Kurt smirked at Rodney over their trays. "The neighbors don't know yet?"

"They don't know what?" Rodney asked.

Kurt laughed. "You and Tim are gay."

Rodney couldn't help laughing himself. "Why would our neighbors suspect? Because we're willing to be seen in public with you?"

*****

Aunt Juergen decided to lease her farm to Rodney and Tim. It was the same "on shares" deal she'd had with the Larsons. It meant the owner of the land and the buildings equally shared the expenses, income and major decisions with those who did the work. It also meant landlords and tenants equally shared good years and bad.

Kurt helped move Rodney and Tim into Aunt Juergen's tenant house.

Kurt's showing up at a time like that proved to the boys' muttering parents what they'd suspected. Henry Reinhart's grandson and that Chris with the Russian or Polish last name had lured their sons into their net. Crosley had been right about them all along.

Aunt Juergen filed petitions in the court in Edinburgh to become Rodney and Tim's legal guardian. Their parents saw the point of not contesting her requests. It got their "queer" sons out of their lives for good. They were glad to let Aunt Juergen take responsibility for them.

She did, too. Her lease required Tim and Rodney to finish high school. It also rewarded them with three-fourths of the net income from the farm as long as they were both students in good standing at Northern in DeKalb.

They could use her car to go to their classes, in high school as well as in college.

Tim could still take the bus to Edinburgh High. But Rodney was finishing his senior year at Kensington. His lunches with Kurt weren't over yet.

*****

Many of the Juergens thought the lease was unduly favorable to the tenants, who were only seventeen.

"But maybe," they said, "Aunt Juergen has a reason for favoring them. People say neither of those boys seems to have much interest in girls."

Kurt enjoyed hearing Arny and Elaine repeat that gossip.

"I think she favors Tim and Rodney," Kurt said, "because she can be herself with them. At long last, she can speak honestly with somebody."

That got Kurt a look from Arny.

"You, too, I suppose?" Arny asked.

"Yeah," Kurt said. "I might be in on that."

Chapter Thirty-Four

Kurt also planned to attend Northern in the fall. He'd live at home with his grandfather and drive back and forth to his classes. He had no doubt he could do as much work on the farm as he was presently doing.

He only needed to put the matter to his grandfather once. Henry agreed to pay Kurt's tuition and other expenses. He'd also let him use his car.

"And if Elaine and Arny complain about it," Henry said, "I'll buy them a new car, the cheapest one Chevrolet makes. For them to use as they see fit. Just to shut them up. My father would be pleased you're going to college."

*****

After supper on a Saturday in late April of 1961, Kurt worked in the hilltop garden Otto had created and Bertha had taken over when she married Henry.

Ten days earlier, the Soviet Union had sent the first human, Yuri Gagarin, into outer space.

The previous day, President Kennedy had taken responsibility for what the media called "a humiliating loss" to Fidel Castro in the Bay of Pigs.

"Victory has a hundred fathers," the president chose to say, "and defeat is an orphan."

Out of the corner of his eye, Kurt watched Arny and Elaine climb the hill, walk past his grandfather's house and come through the orchard toward him.

As they approached, Kurt stopped his spadework and looked at them.

Arny spoke first. "Mom enjoyed working up here spring evenings."

Kurt knew that was true. She'd spent many of those evenings during the last years of her life teaching Kurt how to tend the garden. She called him her "apprentice."

"Yeah," Elaine said, looking at Kurt, "we can get teary-eyed thinking about the good old days. Especially the many days that actually weren't all that good."

"I suppose we can still be grateful," Kurt said, "they weren't all bad."

Elaine didn't know it, but Kurt was quoting a remark his grandmother had made to him one other spring evening regarding the days of the severe winter they'd recently survived.

"Your uncle and I," Elaine continued, "have spent years of our lives working day after day on this damned farm. Forgive us if we feel we've done enough."

"You have every right to feel that way," Kurt agreed. "You've both done more than enough."

"I haven't had a normal life," Elaine said. "Not living on Henry Reinhart's farm. This man I married turned out to be what you and other people like him now choose to call gay. I stayed here anyway, didn't I? I stayed and gave you the care your mother should've given you but didn't because she was a slut."

"And as the son of that slut," Kurt said, "I thank you for what you did for me. Only the goodness of your heart required you to do it."

Elaine chose not to respond to those remarks.

"But as far as my uncle is concerned," Kurt said, "I can't help but note you've chosen to remain with him more than twenty years after you found out he was gay. You didn't have to do that either. I'm quite certain you could've left him, gotten a divorce and started over somewhere else. That being the case, I can only suppose Arny must've been a comfort to you. He's clearly the most loyal friend you'll ever have in this world. Whatever happens from now on, I hope you treat him well."

Arny had tears running down his face.

"You've said enough, Kurt," he managed to say.

*****

Elaine, though, hadn't said enough.

"We'll win," she said to Kurt. "Arny and I will force you to sell your granddad's farm. Someday you'll have to say good-by to all this."

"You know I'll never go along with that," Kurt said. "I'll do whatever it takes to keep this farm together, for as long as I can."

He'd wondered if, when the time came, he'd be able to find a bank willing to lend him the money for a buyout. Not likely, he'd decided, for a buyout big enough to pay his aunt and uncle for half of everything his grandfather owned.

"The law doesn't favor you, Kurt," Elaine said. "By all means, though, play your hand."

"What hand is that?" Kurt asked.

"As your granddad's beloved grandson. Play it out as long as you can. Up here on top of Mount Reinhart. Looking down your noses at everybody else."

Kurt chose not to respond to that.

Elaine smirked. "You've gotten your granddad to go along with whatever you want."

"He and I agree on many things," Kurt said.

Elaine scoffed. "You somehow get everybody to agree with you. You even convinced Aunt Juergen to take on your boyfriends as her tenants. And they're still in high school."

"I didn't have anything to do with that," Kurt said. "And Rodney and Tim aren't my boyfriends."

Elaine laughed again. "Well, go ahead. Do whatever you please. Your affair with Chris was amusing, to say the least. Were they, or weren't they? That sort of talk is always fun."

Kurt hadn't imagined anybody other than Cecil cared enough to wonder about it.

"Someday," Elaine said, "your dreamworld here will come to an end. Arny and I will take our share of the money and live in the Florida sun winter, spring, summer and fall. You can take your share and do whatever the hell you want with it. But you'll have to face it. Your grandfather's precious ill-gotten farm will be gone."

"It wasn't ill-gotten," Kurt said, resuming his work in his garden, "and it won't be gone."

Elaine and Arny looked at one another and wordlessly walked back through the orchard and down the hill to their house.

Where they belonged, Kurt thought. Both of them. Together. Away from him.

*****

Kurt was working in his garden again the next evening when Arny showed up alone.

"I'm sorry," Arny said. "Elaine is right. We want to leave this farm as soon as we can. What you and your granddad say you love so much, Elaine and I despise. It's never brought us anything but unhappiness. We'd like to leave this place tomorrow and never return to it."

"Running away from yourself," Kurt said to his uncle. "That's all you've ever done. Now I'm supposed to believe a move to Florida is going to make you happy? And Elaine as well? Can you try to explain to me how that's supposed to work?"

"It's what Elaine wants, Kurt. And Elaine is all I have."

Kurt noted that Arny had excluded both his father and his nephew from playing any part in what he had.

"And simply because Elaine wants to run off to a place she's never even visited," Kurt asked, "I'm supposed to agree to sell my grandfather's farm?"

"You won't have a choice, Kurt. The lawyer told us that. The probate court will order it sold, whether you want it sold or not."

"If that's true," Kurt said, pointing toward the house where he lived with his grandfather, "then I hope he outlives us all. And if he doesn't, then I'll just have to find some way to keep his farm together."

Kurt pressed his spade into the soil with his foot and resumed his work.

"And if you and Elaine don't like the result and never make it to Florida," he continued, "please remember one thing. I won't give a damn."

After turning over a long row of soil, Kurt looked up from his work.

His uncle once again made no attempt to hide his tears.

"I don't know why you think this farm is so wonderful," Arny said, his voice unsteady. "He had to commit every crime in the book to get it—even murder."

"Murder?" Kurt asked. "Do you really think your own father committed murder?"

Arny wiped his eyes with the sleeve of his shirt.

"Everybody says that, Kurt. You're the only person who doesn't. You're the only person who defends him."

"And I'm also the only person who knows what he's talking about. You and your beloved Elaine sure as hell don't."

His Grandfather's House

*****

In another five weeks the school year would be over for Kurt. So would the spring work.

Then he'd pay another visit to the law library in Edinburgh to figure out a way to stop Elaine and Arny.

Chapter Thirty-Five

During the next, and last, Thursday afternoon in April of 1961, Gwendolyn Smith paid a visit to Kensington High School and asked to see Kurt. The principal excused him from study hall.

Kurt and Gwendolyn spoke together in the grove of oaks and hickories behind the school.

As in the woods on his grandfather's farm, the violets were in bloom.

"Chris called me," Gwendolyn said. "His mother has died."

"I'm very sorry to hear that," Kurt said.

"So am I. But it's just as well, you know. There was nothing the doctors could do for her. She was in constant pain and heavily medicated. Chris and his father were running out of money paying for nurses to care for her when they were at their jobs."

"He told you that?"

"I asked him about it. He answered me honestly. I knew he would."

"He would," Kurt agreed.

"The funeral for his mother is this Saturday," Gwendolyn said. "I intend to drive there early in the morning and come home in the evening. It'll be a day trip."

She stopped for a moment to scrutinize Kurt's face.

"Would you like to go with me?" she asked.

She bit her lower lip when she saw Kurt's tears.

"Chris told me he'd like to see you," she said. "He asked me to let you know that."

*****

Kurt told his grandfather at supper that evening what he intended to do on Saturday.

Henry, who'd chosen not to attend his own wife's funeral, readily agreed his grandson—who'd stormed out of that one—should go to the service for a woman neither of them had met.

And Kurt was a grandson who could get a hell of a lot done on a fair-weather Saturday that time of the year. Plus, he did what he did on his own initiative, without being asked.

*****

During the drive to Chris's hometown, Kurt began to wonder if he was making a serious mistake.

Chris knew Gwendolyn would tell Kurt his mother had died. And, just to be nice, Chris would've thrown in his remark about wanting to see Kurt, whether he actually did or not.

Chris must've found somebody else in the last eleven months, and that person would surely attend the funeral.

Kurt couldn't deny he was curious to find out who the man was. But the prospect of meeting him filled Kurt with dread. The friend's existence would only underscore Kurt's loss.

*****

Kurt hadn't been inside a Roman Catholic church before.

Chris had disassociated himself from his parents' religion when he was still in his early teens, and they hadn't objected.

A priest had offered to perform fellatio on him. Chris told the man the thought of it made him sick to his stomach. The bishop removed the priest for following through on his overtures to other boys.

Now Chris, in the navy blue suit he'd worn at the bank, stood with his father next to his mother's coffin in his parents' church, greeting a long line of mourners.

Chris was the loyal son who'd cared for his dying mother. Many of the people were in tears when they spoke to him and shook his hand.

Gwendolyn had warned Kurt it would be a long day before they'd get a chance to speak with Chris privately. They'd say hello to him in the line, but they'd have to keep moving along. She'd correctly guessed the crowd would be huge. Then they'd sit through the funeral, drive to the cemetery for the burial and come back to the church for the usual meal.

Every attractive young man who spoke with Chris set off an alarm for Kurt. And there were so many in the church that day. Those who looked as if they were still in high school didn't worry Kurt. But those who appeared to be old enough for college—and especially those who weren't with a woman their age—were another story.

When Chris looked down the line and saw him with Gwendolyn,

Kurt guessed what he had to be thinking. Here comes that silly, awkward boy from Kensington. Why didn't he have enough sense to stay home on a sunny spring day and help his grandfather in his fields?

When it was Kurt's turn to shake hands with Chris, he did so with the stiffness of a toy soldier.

But Chris drew Kurt close to him and whispered in his ear.

"I'm damned glad to see you," he said

Then he let Kurt, once again human, go.

*****

During the funeral service and the visit to the cemetery, Kurt still found himself staring at any man he suspected might be the boyfriend.

He wondered if those who caught him staring at them might think he was insane.

But he felt he had to see the man, meet him—and go on to remember him forever with overwhelming, suffocating regret. This would be Kurt's tragedy, one worse than an early death.

*****

Kurt and Gwendolyn ate with the other mourners back at the church.

"It's a waiting game now," Gwendolyn said as they sat down at a table with their food. "We'll be here for a while. Let's be sure to talk with as many people as we can."

Following up on that, she introduced herself and Kurt to the others at their table. She said they were Chris's two best friends during his last year in college, when he lived in what she called "our little paradise on earth," Kensington.

She soon found out who the others at the table were and pried information out of them concerning Chris. She knew all she had to do was express interest in their stories and urge them to continue. She was like a thief in the night among people who left their doors unlocked.

Kurt wondered how many of them had heard about Cecil's outrageous accusations but couldn't dare say they had, not in the presence of the person who must've been Chris's alleged sodomite accomplice.

*****

Late in the afternoon, Gwendolyn was at the head table speaking of financial matters with Chris's father. All the boyfriend suspects had left.

Kurt said good-by to the woman who'd been Chris's history advisor at Northern. She and Kurt had spent a good deal of time talking about a novel they'd both recently read, *To Kill a Mockingbird*.

Chris hugged, shook hands with and said good-by to the last of his aunts and uncles.

Then he invited Gwendolyn and Kurt to his father's house.

*****

Kurt and Chris sat in a pair of ancient, unpainted wooden lawn chairs facing a patch of violets under an oak tree in the backyard.

Chris looked over Kurt in his dark blue suit and smiled.

It was the first suit Kurt had bought. Rodney had convinced him he'd need it for his graduation. Even Kurt's grandfather had promised to attend. As the class valedictorian, Kurt had to give a speech.

"Gwendolyn told me," Chris said, "your cousin Tim and your friend Rodney are Aunt Juergen's new tenants. I was sorry to hear about Eric Larson's father."

Gwendolyn had persuaded her husband to loan Rodney and Tim the money to buy Eric Larson's mother's share of the livestock and machinery. Aunt Juergen had cosigned for them.

"I've been wondering," Chris said, "why neither of those guys became your boyfriend. They're quite good-looking. And if I remember correctly, they're also the same age you are."

"I couldn't be their boyfriend," Kurt said, his voice unsteady. "With both of them, it was never a possibility."

"Why do you say that?"

"You know why."

"I do?"

"Yeah, I agree they're attractive guys. I like them a lot. The only problem with them doing farmwork together is they can't keep their hands off one another."

Chris laughed. "You still haven't answered my question. Why wasn't it possible for you to be their boyfriend?"

"They aren't you."

Chris, no longer laughing, stared at Kurt.

"I'm very sorry," Kurt said, "but I'm still hopelessly in love with you. I'm as crazy about you as my grandfather was about the section of land he thought he had to own. He was obsessed with that, and I'm obsessed with you. You're the only man I want. And I'm not ready to settle for anybody else. Maybe I'll never be able to do that."

Chris took a deep breath.

"Don't you have a boyfriend?" Kurt asked.

"No, I don't."

"I can't understand why you don't," Kurt said. "You're the most beautiful man on the planet. You're far better-looking than that guy you helped put in the White House. Far more thoughtful, too, I'd say."

Chris chose not to respond to those remarks.

"So why don't you have a boyfriend?" Kurt asked.

"I've been waiting for you."

If Chris had pulled out a gun and taken a shot at Kurt, he wouldn't have surprised him more.

"I'll be honest with you, Kurt. I've never done anything with another guy."

"Neither have I."

"Then why don't we make a date to take care of that?"

"Whatever date we choose, it won't be soon enough for me."

"Okay, in the middle of May, on the sixteenth, you'll be eighteen. At the end of the month you'll graduate from high school."

"That's right," Kurt said. "So there won't be anything stopping us? Only that stupid infamous-crime-against-nature law?"

"I've got some news for you. There's a bill in the legislature. It's a whole new criminal code some professors dreamed up. It'll do away with that law. No other state has done it yet. If the bill passes, it'll make gay sex legal in Illinois. Whatever you and I do will be legal."

"We'll be able to love one another," Kurt asked, "without risking a prison sentence?"

"That's right. When does Kensington High hold its graduation ceremony this year?"

"Monday, May 29."

"Ours is the same day. I'll come to see you Memorial Day."

Memorial Day was on a Tuesday that year.

"And if your grandfather doesn't mind," Chris said, "I'll plan to stay overnight with you."

"He won't mind. And I won't let you do anything else."

Chapter Thirty-Six

Chris and his father couldn't pay his mother's medical bills. Two doctors and a hospital had already filed judgment liens against the house that Chris's parents had used all their savings to buy when they quit farming and moved to Rockford.

The doctors and hospital had opted not to foreclose on their liens as long as Chris's mother was in the house. The media might've sent reporters and photographers—people her son knew—to be present when the sheriff's deputies removed a dying woman from her home.

At one point during Gwendolyn's conversation with Chris's father after the funeral, Kurt had heard her speak of the matter.

"I'll get you a loan to pay off those judgments," she'd said. "I'll do it if I have to cosign for it myself."

The banks in the Rockford area had turned Chris and his father down when they applied for a mortgage loan. The bank officers said putting Chris on the deed and making him liable for the debt along with his father wouldn't help. Chris still had his student loans to pay off.

Gwendolyn talked Chester into offering Chris and his father a loan from the Kensington State Bank. And she wouldn't have to cosign after all. Henry Reinhart agreed to do it.

*****

On Memorial Day, Chris arrived in time to eat lunch with Kurt and Henry.

That afternoon he filled in for Arny, who'd chosen to take the holiday off.

Henry, Kurt and Chris circled the farm with one tractor pulling the hay mower and the other the hay wagon. They cut the grass growing along all four roadsides, forked it onto the wagon as high as they could, and hauled several loads of it back to the barn. The cattle would feed on it the next rainy day.

The purpose of their work, Henry told Chris, was to keep weeds like thistle, mustard and morning glory from taking root in the roadsides and spreading from there into his clean fields. A regularly clipped roadside wasn't for the benefit of passersby, he said, but for the farmer who worked the fields behind it.

Whatever its purpose, the result was a one-square-mile northern Illinois farm within a necklace of lawn as crew-cut as the heads of the three persons who'd manicured it.

*****

Kurt and Chris said good night to Henry as soon as they finished washing, drying and putting away the supper dishes. They showered and hurried up the stairs in towels to Kurt's floor.

When they reached the west bedroom Kurt slept in that time of the year, they took off their towels and hugged one another as if they might never let go again.

"I'm damned glad," Kurt said, "you made me wait for this."

"And I'm damned glad," Chris said, "you waited."

*****

Soon after they rose from the bed the next morning, Chris agreed he'd take the teaching assistant position at Northern. He'd also live with Kurt in his grandfather's house.

The next rainy day came later that week. While the cattle munched on the roadside grass, Kurt and Chris drove to Rockford, ate lunch with Chris's father, packed Chris's clothes and other belongings in the trunk and backseat of Henry's car, and returned to Mount Reinhart.

Most of their work was loading and unloading the books, many of them hardcover, Chris said he couldn't live without.

But Kurt was more than willing to help accomplish that.

"It proves," he told Chris, "how much I love a man who loves books."

*****

One afternoon when Henry had nothing more urgent for them to do, Kurt and Chris hoed weeds in the garden. Kurt uprooted a thistle, worked it into the soil, and put to Chris another question he'd decided he could leave unasked no longer.

"Why didn't you get a political job? After what you did for those people in the election?"

Chris stopped hoeing and looked at Kurt.

"Not a thing for you?" Kurt asked. "No federal job? No state job? Why is that? Don't they appreciate what you did?"

"Do you really want to know?" Chris asked.

"Yeah, I do."

"Do you really want to hear something you won't like hearing?"

"Just tell me," Kurt said. "I'm eighteen now. I'm a big boy."

"Okay. They checked into my background. They found out a minister at a church in Kensington, Illinois, had made some allegations from his pulpit. He'd claimed a college student living in that town and working for the local bank was committing the infamous crime against nature with a sixteen-year-old boy."

Kurt shook his head. "That's what I wanted. But thanks to you, it never happened."

"They agreed the minister was a crackpot. They also said they believed me when I told them you and I were only book-reading, chess-playing friends. Still, they couldn't take the slightest chance something like what I was accused of would turn out to be true."

"I really fucked things up for you."

"No, you didn't," Chris said, dropping his hoe and giving Kurt a hug. "You were just what I needed. I realized I didn't want any of their jobs. I wanted you. I wanted to live a quiet life somewhere with you. You saved me from them—from their world."

*****

Henry paid Chris generously for the work he did on the farm.

After Chris moved into the house with Kurt and Henry, Arny rarely showed up for work. But he offered to help Kurt feed the livestock the afternoon Henry and Chris went to the Kensington State Bank to close on the deal to save the house in Rockford.

Soon after Arny began working, he set his pails down for a breather and looked at Kurt.

"Elaine and I don't feel at home here anymore," he said.

"What are you talking about?" Kurt asked, pausing his own work.

"Isn't it obvious, Kurt? Elaine and I are your backward relatives. We've accomplished nothing in our lives, and we never will. We shouldn't live on the same farm with you anymore. We can see what you've done with the old man. He loves you and Chris. He's never come close to loving me and Elaine."

Kurt didn't like those remarks and thought it best to ignore them.

"Elaine and I just want our share of everything," Arny said. "After the cash-out."

"You mean," Kurt said, "after your father dies. Even though we can't possibly know when that will happen. He could still be alive twenty years from now. I don't understand why you and Elaine worry so much about what's going to take place after that."

"I'll tell you why. Because you don't want us to sell this goddamned cattle-shit, hog-shit farm a crazy man put together."

Kurt glared at his uncle. "You and Elaine can goddamn the cow shit and hog shit all you want. But the crazy man and I believe it's precious. It's why his crops grow so well. It's why he owns a section of land to spread it on. I'm sorry you and Elaine don't see it that way."

"No, we don't see it that way, Kurt. We just want our share of everything in money."

"All you and Elaine want out of your lives on this farm is money?"

"Looking forward to that money is all we've got left in our lives."

Kurt picked up his pails and resumed feeding his grandfather's livestock.

*****

One rainy day late in June, Kurt and Chris went to visit the library in Edinburgh.

They learned the law in Illinois hadn't changed since Otto died in 1911 and left everything he owned to Henry.

Parents could exclude their children from their estates, but it had to be done in a will. Otherwise, Elaine and Arny's lawyer was right. Half of Henry's estate would go to Arny, the other half to Kurt.

"Are you sure," Chris asked, "your grandfather doesn't have a will?"

Chris, who was driving his car, stared past the windshield wipers into the rain.

"I've never seen one among his papers," Kurt replied. "I have access to all of them. He's never said anything to me about a will."

"I think you should tell him."

"Tell him what? The Illinois inheritance law hasn't changed in fifty years? He probably assumes, as we did, it hasn't."

Chris kept his eyes on the road in front of them.

"We should've waited out this damned storm at Rodney and Tim's," Kurt said. "We didn't have to hurry off. We should've had another beer with them. They're in love with you as much as I am."

"You know what you've got to tell your grandfather," Chris said. "Your aunt and uncle want to sell his farm, and you want to keep it. He needs to know that."

Kurt also stared at the road ahead.

"I should let my grandfather know," he asked, "my aunt and uncle are traitors?"

Chapter Thirty-Seven

That evening during supper Kurt told his grandfather Arny and Elaine had assured him they'd force the sale of his farm.

"When you're no longer around," Kurt explained, "to keep them from doing it."

Henry looked at Kurt as if his grandson had revealed the Third World War had begun.

"Arny agrees with that?" Henry asked.

"He says he'd leave for Florida tomorrow," Kurt replied. "He's had enough of this goddamned cattle-shit, hog-shit farm."

"That's the way he's talking?" Henry asked.

"For some time now," Kurt said. "I should've told you."

"And you want to keep the farm?"

"Of course I do," Kurt said. "You spent your life putting it together. Why would I give a moment's thought to selling it? I want to live the rest of my life in this house, on this farm."

Kurt turned to Chris.

"With this man," he added.

Henry looked at Chris. "Is that what you want?"

"Yes, I do," Chris replied. "As long as your grandson will have me."

"And that," Kurt said, "will be until the day I die."

*****

Henry spent the next rainy afternoon in an attorney's office in Edinburgh.

Before he'd left, Kurt and Chris told him to take his time with the lawyer figuring out what he should do. They'd handle the chores and have supper waiting whenever he came home.

Chris thought the lawyer would set up a trust with instructions to the trustee not to sell the farm unless all the beneficiaries agreed to it. The trustee would be a bank. The beneficiaries would be Arny, Elaine and Kurt.

"Or something like that," Chris said.

*****

"At least five gay men have lived their entire lives on this farm."

"Five?" Chris asked. "Their entire lives?"

"Just think about it," Kurt said. "My great-grandfather Gus Hagenbach, my great-uncle Conrad Reinhart, our neighbor Albert Rauenthaler, my uncle Arny, and me. That's five."

"And four of those gay men," Chris said, "weren't very gay at all."

"That was then," Kurt said. "We're living now. We can be gay. We can be happy."

Kurt and Chris lay naked on the bed in the room facing west and north upstairs, the same bed Henry and Conrad had slept in. The room had a peaked ceiling and no attic space above it.

Kurt and Chris could hear the rain falling on the roof. They'd chosen not to waste the afternoon Henry had picked to see an attorney.

"Besides," Kurt said, "it's patronizing for us to assume they were unhappy. The original three had their Saturday nights together. They lit candles. They drank booze. They threatened to kill my grandfather. That must've been fun. I mean, some good-looking straight asshole haughtily turns you down. And you and your friends come right back at that fucker with a death threat. Wow."

"They kept the curtains closed, too, didn't they?"

Kurt laughed. "They didn't have a house on Mount Reinhart where they could leave the windows open, do whatever they pleased and not worry about anybody seeing them do it."

"What about your uncle?" Chris asked. "Is he happy?"

"He likes watching television with Elaine. You should see them in their kitchen when they're making their meals and snacks. I'd call that happy. I can't imagine why they think they need to go to Florida to do what they do."

Chris got up from the bed.

Every time Kurt saw that naked, twenty-three-year-old body, toned in the gym as well as on the farm, it was like taking a bullet to his heart.

"Time for chores," Chris said, handing Kurt his shorts. "I bet we've got some hungry cattle and hogs waiting for us. I can't imagine they wanted to go out in the rain today any more than we did."

*****

His Grandfather's House

After supper that evening, Henry showed Kurt and Chris his will.

He said Kurt should keep it with his other papers. The lawyer in Edinburgh had a copy.

The will was only two paragraphs long.

In the first paragraph, Henry named Kurt John Reinhart executor of his estate—unless at the time of Henry's death Kurt hadn't yet "reached majority."

In other words, Henry explained, if Kurt wasn't twenty-one yet.

If he wasn't, the executor would be Gwendolyn Smith.

"She agreed to that?" Kurt asked.

"The lawyer called and spoke with her himself," his grandfather replied.

The second paragraph was even shorter than the first. "I give, devise and bequeath to my grandson, Kurt John Reinhart, all of my estate, both real and personal, to which I may be entitled at the time of my death, and wheresoever the same may be situated."

Kurt and Chris silently read the paragraph several times.

Kurt looked across the dining room table at his grandfather.

"You can't do this," he said.

Henry laughed. "The lawyer says I can."

"You're not leaving anything to Arny and Elaine," Kurt said.

"That's exactly, to the penny," Henry said, "what I think they deserve."

Kurt scowled at his grandfather. "They've worked hard on this farm. Not recently maybe. But they used to. They both worked hard. They did what you asked them to do. They're counting on Arny's inheritance as the payoff for what they've done."

Henry smiled at his grandson. "That will be your problem, your decision to make. If, after I'm dead, you feel Arny and Elaine need to be paid off for what they've done on this farm, you can give them whatever you please. That's how the lawyer explained it to me."

"I told you," Kurt said, "I'd keep the farm together. I'd continue to pension them off the way you've done. And I'd let them go on living in their house without paying rent. But they want a lot more than that. They want to start a new life down where they won't have to suffer through another winter. They want to buy an expensive place on the beach somewhere. They want enough money in the bank to live on.

They won't have any other income. They want to dine out every night. They want to drive around in an expensive car. They say their half of everything entitles them to live any way they please. To give them what they want, I'd have to sell the farm. And you know I'd never do that."

Once again, Henry smiled, as if he took pleasure in his grandson's obvious pain.

"You'll have some big decisions to make," he said. "The same as I did when I inherited my father's farm. But I trust you'll make the right decisions. I assume Chris will help you."

"I intend to," Chris said. "But I think you're right to trust Kurt."

*****

Henry, Kurt and Chris spent the next Saturday baling hay. In the field, Henry drove the tractor pulling the baler and the wagon behind it. Kurt and Chris, both shirtless, both wearing metal-button 501 Levi's, were on the wagon stacking the bales.

After Henry drove the loaded wagon back to the barn with the other tractor, he placed the bales on the lower end of his conveyor. At the other end, in the hayloft, Kurt and Chris again stacked the bales.

On one of their trips to the barn, Arny was waiting for them. He and Elaine had returned from a shopping trip to Kensington.

He asked to speak with Kurt alone.

"We're busy right now," Kurt said. "We've got a wagonload of hay to put in the barn."

"Go ahead and talk with your uncle," Chris said to Kurt. "I'm sure I can keep up with your granddad all by myself."

Henry laughed at that.

Kurt knew his grandfather would slow things down at his end.

Chapter Thirty-Eight

Kurt and Arny only had to go as far as the chicken coop to speak freely. Neither Chris nor Henry could hear them above the clatter and whine of the conveyor.

"Everybody knows what you've done," Arny said. "They're all talking about it in Kensington. Elaine and I have never been more embarrassed. Why didn't you at least tell me?"

"What have I done?" Kurt asked.

"What have you done? You know goddamn well what you've done."

"I really don't know what you're talking about. Has somebody seen Chris and me in the woods? If so, all I can say is, any person who saw us had to be a trespasser."

"This is about the will, Kurt. Don't tell me you don't know about it. You talked your grandfather into leaving the farm and everything else he owns to you. Elaine and I won't get a dime. You've done the same damned thing with him he did with his father."

"I do know about the will," Kurt said. "It was his idea. I didn't ask him to do it. I told him he shouldn't leave everything to me. But what have you and Elaine got to worry about? If I inherit everything when he dies, I'll take care of you both. You know I will."

"But you won't sell the farm and split the proceeds with us."

"That's right. I won't."

"Elaine doesn't like this."

"Why don't you go see your lawyer?"

"We did. This very day. He told us we're screwed. There's nothing we can do."

Kurt looked past his uncle. Miles in the distance, somewhere in the next county it seemed, blue sky and green land clung to each other like lovers.

"Why does everybody know about the will?" Kurt asked. "I thought lawyers were supposed to keep their clients' business confidential."

"It must've been the lawyer's secretary," Arny replied. "She used to work at Sears. Back when Elaine worked there."

"The lawyer's secretary told people about the will?"

"Nobody can prove it. But she's the one who must've done it."

"Why would she do such a thing?"

Arny sighed. "She hates Elaine and me. She wants to humiliate us."

Arny was in tears again.

"She wanted to marry me," he said. "You don't have to believe this, but people used to think I was a good-looking man."

"I know you were. I've seen the pictures Grandma took of you."

"The lawyer's secretary thinks Elaine stole me away from her. She still talks about it. She tells people she could've given me kids and made me happy. But Elaine couldn't."

"People hold Elaine responsible for her and you not having children?"

"Of course they do. They always blame the woman for that. Even when she's married to a faggot who can't get it up with her. A queer too damned stupid to admit that's what he is."

Bare and sweaty as he was, Kurt took his uncle in his arms.

"I'm sorry," he said. "I'm sorry for what you and Elaine have had to go through."

*****

At supper that evening, Kurt duly reported to his grandfather and Chris what Arny had told him. Everybody in the world who knew who Henry Reinhart was knew about his will.

"That's an outrage," Chris told Henry. "Your lawyer has breached his duty to you. He should know better than to employ a secretary who exposes his clients' business to the public. You should make a complaint against him. I'll call the bar association first thing on Monday and find out how you do it. I'm certain the lawyer and his secretary weren't supposed to tell anybody what was in your will."

Henry looked at Chris and smiled, no doubt grateful his grandson had chosen so well.

"But why should I care?" Henry asked. "The lawyer's secretary is still in love with my handsome son. I can't blame her. She certainly doesn't deserve to be punished for it."

Chris chose not to disagree with any of those remarks.

"To tell you the truth," Henry continued, "I feel the lawyer's secretary has done me a great favor. She let the world know I'm leaving my farm to Kurt. Who could ask for more than that?"

"She also let Arny and Elaine know," Kurt said.

His Grandfather's House

"I'm glad they know," his grandfather said. "I vote we leave the secretary alone. How could this world get by without gossip? It's the lubricant that keeps everything else moving."

*****

The next day, the Reverend Cecil Crosley delivered a sermon on the duties parents owe their children. He spoke in particular of "a person who owns a large farm in this county but sees no need to acknowledge the existence of God by attending church."

That person's most recent outrage was his execution of a will that gave none of his estate to his only living son and daughter-in-law.

He'd chosen instead to leave everything to his grandson. And everybody knew that "atheist queer" was as defiant of God as his grandfather was.

The grandson had even taken into his grandfather's house his male consort in evil. They lived together as if they could do what lawfully wedded men and women did.

"And the grandfather lets them do it under his roof!" Cecil boomed. "As if God and His laws don't exist!"

Those were the last words Cecil spoke. He fell forward, clinging to his lectern.

Cecil died in the Edinburgh Community Hospital that afternoon. He was eighty-three years old. The coroner once again determined cardiac arrest had caused a death in Kensington township.

Cecil's congregants agreed his many trips to Las Vegas, which he'd attempted to pass off as visits to his daughter and her family in Nebraska, had taken their toll.

Neither his nor the church's accounts at the Kensington State Bank held a fraction of the money needed to pay off the church mortgage. The bank would have to foreclose on it.

Many of the faithful began to fear only an act of divine intervention would keep the sheriff from selling what Cecil had called his "House of God" to the highest bidder.

*****

Kurt, his grandfather and Chris were finishing their supper when

Arny burst into the kitchen without bothering to knock on the door. Out of breath after climbing the hill that warm July evening, he dropped into the empty fourth chair at the table as if it had always been his.

"Elaine went to Edinburgh this afternoon," he said. "She bought two pistols. She showed them to me. She's got some ammo, too."

"Do you know why she bought the guns?" Kurt asked.

Arny looked at Kurt and blinked his eyes.

"She says a father who leaves his son out of his will deserves to be shot. She learned how to use those guns, too. She took target practice right there where she bought them. They told her she must have excellent eyesight. She's never worn glasses. Not even for reading."

For a long time after that, nobody chose to speak.

Chris, looking at Arny, broke the silence.

"Do you feel safe with Elaine?" he asked.

"Of course I do," Arny replied. "She hasn't threatened to kill me."

"You don't want to stay here with us?" Kurt asked.

"No, I have to go home," Arny said. "I don't want her to find out I came up here. I've never seen her so angry."

He put his hands on the table and pushed himself up from his chair.

"I just wanted you to know about the guns."

*****

Chris called the sheriff's office. The deputy he asked to speak with, the former Kensington High quarterback, called the sheriff himself, who was at home eating dinner with his wife and grandchildren.

The sheriff denied out of hand the request Chris had made.

"If Reinhart needs protection from his daughter-in-law," the sheriff told the deputy, "tell him he'll have to hire a security guard. I'm sure he's got enough money to pay for one."

The sheriff paused to laugh.

"Or he can ask his Kennedy friends for a loan."

The deputy repeated those remarks to Chris. They'd played against one another in the state football tournaments in the autumns of 1954 and 1955.

"I'm not surprised," Kurt said.

"Why do you say that?" Chris asked.

"Guess who the father of the current sheriff was," Kurt said. "The fired deputy who won his first election for sheriff by insisting Henry Reinhart should've been prosecuted for murdering his brother."

Kurt, his grandfather and Chris locked shut all the first-floor windows as well as the doors. They agreed at least one of them would remain awake in the kitchen throughout the night, near the telephone— to call the deputy back immediately, as he'd advised them, in case anything at all happened.

Henry retrieved his shotgun from the basement and cleaned and oiled it. He left it fully loaded on the kitchen table.

"To be used as needed," he said.

Chapter Thirty-Nine

In the morning, Henry took his gun with him when he started down the path to the barn to do the chores. He'd made Kurt and Chris promise to remain a safe distance away from him.

"The quarrel is between Elaine and me," he'd said. "And this old man isn't afraid to die. But you've got your lives to live. I don't want either of you taking a bullet meant for me."

As soon as Kurt reached the back door steps, he saw Arny shuffle out from behind Otto's lilac bush.

"Call the sheriff," Kurt said to Chris, who was following him. "And stay in the house."

Henry raised his shotgun and took aim at Arny.

Elaine was behind Arny. She was using him as her shield.

She held one of her pistols in her left hand with its muzzle against Arny's back. She held her other pistol in her right hand resting on Arny's shoulder. She had that one aimed at Henry.

"It's time," she said, "to burn your goddamned will."

"I'm not burning my will," Henry said. "I want it just as it is."

"Tell Kurt to get your will," Elaine said. "Arny says he's got it. Tell him to bring some matches. You can set it on fire. Our lawyer says that'll take care of the matter."

"I'm not burning my will," Henry said.

"You'll either burn the will," Elaine said, "or I'll put a bullet through your goddamned head."

Kurt didn't doubt she would.

"I'll get the will," he said.

"Thank you, Kurt," Arny said.

"Leave that will right where it is," Henry said to Kurt, without taking his eyes off Elaine. "I'm not going to burn it. If she wants to shoot me, let her do it. You might have to testify at her trial, though, you saw her do it. Are you ready for that?"

"Get the will, Kurt," Elaine said.

"Get the will," Arny pleaded.

"Stay right where you are," Henry told his grandson.

Chris had the back door and all the kitchen windows wide open. He held the phone receiver up so that a deputy in the sheriff's office could hear the Reinharts yelling at one another.

"Get the will," Elaine said to her nephew. "Otherwise, I'll shoot your granddad dead."

Kurt didn't move.

Elaine took her eyes off Henry and looked at Kurt.

As if he'd fallen into a paralytic dream state, Kurt remained where he was.

Elaine began moving the gun in her right hand to take aim at Kurt.

And that changed everything for all of them forever.

She should've known Henry would never let her aim her pistol at his grandson.

Henry fired his gun.

Arny dropped to his knees. Blood spurted from multiple wounds to his head and body.

Elaine, unscathed, fired her pistol at Henry.

At that same moment, though, Henry fired the second round of his shotgun.

Elaine's bullet hit Henry in his forehead above his left eye.

Dropping her weapons as she fell to the ground, Elaine soon bled from as many wounds as Arny did.

*****

Kurt and Chris attempted to keep Henry, Elaine and Arny alive. They used their own tee shirts and dozens of kitchen towels to stanch their bleeding.

But even before the sheriff's deputies came running up the hill with their guns drawn, Kurt could tell his aunt, uncle and grandfather were dead.

"Oh, Jesus!" Kurt and Chris heard the other quarterback cry out.

He was the first deputy to reach the top of the hill and see five people—two living, three dead—covered with blood.

*****

Several hundred media people, including reporters from all the Chicago television stations, arrived at the scene of the violence in rural Kensington township in Lafayette County. The carnage involved three individuals who'd been in the news before—Henry, Chris and Kurt.

The sheriff's deputies estimated a crowd of two to three

thousand onlookers had gathered to observe the proceedings. After all, one of the three people shot to death was Henry Reinhart.

The reporters interviewed the sheriff outside the back door of Henry's house on the hill, near where the first deputies on the scene had discovered the three bodies.

Viewers could also see the water tower in Kensington against a cloudless sky behind him.

The sheriff confirmed the facts of the case. An argument had led to Henry Reinhart's first shooting his son, Arnold Reinhart, and then his daughter-in-law, Elaine Reinhart, with his shotgun. During the gunplay, Elaine fired her pistol once. Her bullet struck Henry in his head.

Two other persons were present during the shootings, the sheriff explained. One was Henry's grandson, Kurt Reinhart. The other was the man who lived with Kurt and Henry, Christopher Stefanovski. Neither Kurt nor Mr. Stefanovski had taken part in the shooting. A deputy had heard, over the telephone, the shouting among the Reinharts and the shots they'd fired.

"We consider this a triple homicide," the sheriff concluded, reading from a prepared statement in his trembling hands. "Both suspects are dead. No charges will be filed."

Rodney and Tim had let the media know the sheriff, who was said to be seeking reelection in 1962, had refused to supply any protection for the Reinhart family. And in doing so, he'd sarcastically referred to their support for Kennedy the previous November.

One well-known television reporter from Chicago asked the sheriff whether Lafayette County residents who voted for Democrats could expect to receive the same protection from his office that Republicans did. After more questioning on that issue by other reporters, the sheriff apologized to the Reinhart family and their friends for what he agreed was a thoughtless remark.

*****

Several times, Rodney, Tim and Gwendolyn told the media people Kurt and Chris wouldn't come out of the house to speak with them. Just as many times, the reporters insisted they wouldn't leave until they'd heard from the two eyewitnesses to the shootings.

Kurt and Chris decided they could no longer expect their friends to bear their burden. Nor could they ask the sheriff to attempt to remove the huge crowd outside their back door.

At the request of the television cameramen, Kurt and Chris stood in the early afternoon sunshine where the sheriff had made his statement, with the house on Mount Reinhart behind them.

Providing detail after detail, some of them delivered tearfully, Kurt described how his three closest relatives had died that morning. He also explained the argument over his grandfather's will that led to the violence.

"Kurt," the celebrity television reporter asked, "do you believe the sheriff did all he could do to protect your family and prevent the deaths of your relatives?"

"I don't blame the sheriff," Kurt replied. "I don't blame him for anything he did or didn't do regarding my family. He can't provide round-the-clock protection for every family in the county threatened with violence. Why should he have felt any need to favor mine?"

The sheriff and his deputies stared at Kurt. It was obvious they hadn't anticipated that reply from him.

The publisher of the *Edinburgh Times*, who'd led the negotiations with Rodney, Tim and Gwendolyn, was ready to pursue another line of inquiry with Kurt.

"Many of your neighbors here seem to think," he said, "your grandfather committed murder, arson and other crimes to acquire the farm he left you in his will. Would you care to comment?"

The publisher and Kurt both knew he wouldn't face a lawsuit for the remark preceding his question. Only the person he might've slandered, Henry, could've sued him, and he was dead.

"Any neighbors or other people who say that," Kurt replied, "are wrong. You and I have looked into everything he's been accused of. And neither of us has found any evidence he ever did anything illegal. You know as well as I do, he had no need to murder his brother. He was going to win the will-contest case his brother had filed against him. You wrote the articles at the time explaining everything. It's too bad nobody paid any attention to what you said. My grandfather's father knew what he was doing when he signed his will and left his farm to his only child who wasn't an alcoholic. He told the witnesses to his will what he was doing. He knew all three of them. They were bank employees. He asked them about their families. He signed his will as they watched. They were prepared to testify in court for my grandfather. Conrad's attorney hadn't found anybody to testify against them."

As Kurt spoke, the sheriff began walking up the hill toward him and Chris.

Kurt had one last thing to say. "Nobody except my grandmother has ever known my grandfather as well as I have. And I'm as certain as I can be he never would've murdered his brother or anybody else to obtain a farm."

"What about this morning, Kurt?" the publisher asked. "Didn't your grandfather shoot and kill his own son and daughter-in-law, your uncle and aunt?"

"Wait a minute," Chris interjected. "You heard Kurt describe what happened this morning. His grandfather had a reason to do what he did. And a damned good reason, I'd say. His daughter-in-law was moving her pistol to take aim at Kurt. Mr. Reinhart killed his son and his daughter-in-law, and got killed himself, in order to save his grandson's life. I want people to know that's what happened this morning. I saw it myself. Kurt's aunt committed murder this morning. What his grandfather did wasn't murder."

When Chris finished his remarks, the sheriff was standing next to Kurt.

The publisher turned to the sheriff. "Do you have something more to say?"

"I do," the sheriff said, turning to Kurt, "if you want me to. It's what my father told me about the death of your grandfather's brother. My father made me promise him I'd never tell anybody else what he told me until Henry Reinhart was no longer alive. Rightly or wrongly, I've kept that promise. I've never told a single soul, not even my wife or any of my children."

Kurt nodded his head. "I'm eager to hear what your father told you."

The sheriff turned to face the reporters and cameras. "First, let me say this. Contrary to what some of you might think, I don't intend to run for reelection next year. I do intend to enjoy the remainder of my years with my wife and our children and grandchildren."

The publisher of the *Edinburgh Times* was impatient.

"What did your father tell you?" he asked the sheriff.

"When my father found Henry's brother, Conrad, he was still

alive," the sheriff replied. "He only had moments to live, though, and he knew it. He'd taken a battering in that flood. He was bleeding from at least a dozen wounds. The coroner said he drowned, but his injuries were what did him in. He could scarcely make himself heard, but he mumbled to my father he was glad he'd pushed his brother, Henry, into the creek. And he hoped to God he'd killed him."

The publisher's surprise was evident. "Conrad admitted pushing Henry into the creek?"

The sheriff nodded his head. "He'd used some excuse to get Henry to go down to the creek with him. Then he maneuvered behind him and gave him a shove."

Kurt looked at the publisher. "That's what my grandfather told me, too. And that's why one of his sisters told you he was soaked that morning. My grandmother also saw him soaked."

The night Kurt and Chris had read his will, Henry gave in to Kurt's demands and told him, as well as Chris, the truth about Conrad's death.

"How did Conrad end up in the creek?" the publisher asked.

Kurt and Chris knew this was the most important question of them all.

"Henry reached out at the last moment," the sheriff replied, "and pulled Conrad into the water with him. My father wasn't sure whether Henry did that in an attempt to save himself or to retaliate for what Conrad had done to him. But that's how they both ended up in the creek."

Kurt looked at the publisher. "My grandfather said he did it to save himself, but Conrad was too hungover that morning to maintain his footing on the wet, slippery ground."

The publisher turned to the sheriff. "Conrad hoped he'd killed Henry?"

"Conrad felt certain he'd killed Henry," the sheriff said. "Neither of them could swim."

"They couldn't," Kurt said. "My grandfather fought like hell anyway and never got swept into the main current. He was twenty-three. The neighbors said he was as strong as an ox then."

The publisher turned to the sheriff again. "Why didn't your father tell the public the truth? He told me he'd found Conrad dead. That's what he told everybody else, too."

"My father didn't blame Conrad for what he'd done," the sheriff replied. "He thought Conrad and his sisters had been cheated out of their shares of their father's farm, the same as my father thought he'd been cheated out of his share of his father's farm."

"The truth," Kurt said, "wouldn't have done my grandfather any good anyway."

"That's right," the sheriff said. "My father told me he was actually doing Henry a favor."

"He was," Kurt said. "That's why my grandfather himself never gave anybody a true account of what happened that day. He knew it would've gotten him indicted for murder. He'd have to explain to a jury in detail what had happened. The jurors might've refused to believe a man who'd supposedly cheated his brother and sisters out of his father's farm. They might've refused to believe he was merely reaching out to his brother to save himself. They might've believed he pulled his brother into the creek to die with him. They couldn't penalize Conrad for what he'd done that day. He was dead. But they could've punished my grandfather. They might've believed he deserved a guilty verdict for stealing his father's farm. Maybe even, at twenty-three, sent to the electric chair to die for a crime he didn't commit."

The publisher turned to the sheriff once more. "Then why did your father tell me and everybody else the state's attorney should've prosecuted Henry Reinhart for murder?"

The sheriff shrugged his shoulders. "My father was no saint. He was out to cause trouble for the politicians in charge of things in Lafayette County. He knew the state's attorney didn't have enough evidence to prosecute Reinhart. He didn't want to see him prosecuted anyway. That would've robbed him of his claim that the bigshots were letting a man get away with murder."

"Yeah," Kurt said, "my grandfather knew your father was playing a political game. But he didn't care what other people thought of him anyway, as long as they didn't put him in prison. He cared about me, though, and I loved him. I'm damned glad he was my grandfather. I'm extremely sorry I'll have to live the rest of my life without him."

*****

Kurt and Chris once again appeared in photos on the front pages of the Chicago-area newspapers, but this time they were in them together.

The lengthy headline the *Edinburgh Times* publisher chose to place above the photo of them, along with photos of Henry, Arny and Elaine that Kurt had given him, revealed his own obsession.

"THREE MORE DEAD IN FIFTY-YEAR-OLD FARM FAMILY TRAGEDY."

Chapter Forty

Kurt buried his grandfather, uncle and aunt with his eight other Reinhart relatives in the orchard on the hill. The only persons present for the burials other than Kurt and Chris were Rodney, Tim, Gwendolyn and the elderly Gibson brothers, Sam and Earl.

Deputy sheriffs, at Kurt's request and with the former Kensington quarterback in charge, kept the media and the neighbors off the island in the prairie his grandfather had created.

The deputies didn't have to use force. All they had to do was stand along the road and motion to the curious passersby in their cars to drive on.

*****

On July 28, 1961, the governor of Illinois signed into law the new criminal code that repealed the infamous crime against nature. It would take effect on January 1, 1962.

*****

On August 13, 1961, the rulers of East Germany, with the permission of their overlords in Moscow, began erecting the Berlin Wall.

*****

Kurt and Chris told Rodney and Tim about their plans for a roadside stand.

Even before Henry had died, Kurt and Chris had begun restoration of Otto Reinhart's orchard, vineyard and berry patches.

"We'll sell fruits and vegetables at the very spot my great-grandfather did," Kurt said.

"What makes you think you can compete with the supermarkets?" Rodney asked.

Kurt scoffed. "What makes you think we can't? Our produce will taste better than theirs. It'll be less expensive, too. We won't have to pick it before it's ripe and pay to transport it thousands of miles in refrigerated railroad cars and trucks."

*****

A probate judge appointed Gwendolyn Smith to be the executor of Henry's estate as well as Kurt's legal guardian until he turned twenty-one.

The judge also had to decide upon Kurt's petition to include Chis as an owner of the farm and the bank accounts.

Kurt and Chris wore their blue suits for the hearing, at Gwendolyn's request.

"They both grew up the only children in their families," she told the judge from the witness stand. "After they met, they entered into a brotherly relationship, becoming the siblings they never had but always apparently needed."

Kurt looked at Chris out of the corner of his eye and stifled a laugh. Brothers didn't do what they did in the upper rooms of his grandfather's house.

"Now the two of them are working the farm together," Gwendolyn continued. "Kurt wants to make certain that if anything happens to him, the property will go to Chris and not to distant relatives he scarcely knows. I strongly believe you should let Kurt do this and give him peace of mind. Especially in view of what happened to his family."

Gwendolyn and Kurt's lawyer looked at the judge and shrugged.

Kurt and Chris had driven through Kensington on their way to Edinburgh that autumn morning. The demolition work on the Kensington Christian Church had begun. The Kensington State Bank had bought the property in order to construct a banking facility bigger and more modern than its present building. It would also have a more central location in the town.

A group of church members had attempted to raise enough money to save the church. Ten minutes into the bidding at the sheriff's sale, it was obvious they'd failed.

The *Edinburgh Times* quoted Chester Smith as saying Kensington needed a new bank building more than it did a revival of Cecil Crosley's "decrepit" church.

When Chris got to the witness stand, at the request of the judge, he was blunt.

"I'm going along with Kurt," he said, "but only because he

240

insists on it."

"You wouldn't want the property," the judge asked, "if anything happened to Kurt?"

"I'd keep the property together as a farm," Chris replied. "Kurt knows I'd never sell it. That's what he wants."

"Then why do you have any reservations about this?"

Chris looked at Kurt and shook his head. "Kurt's only eighteen. He could change his mind about the person he wants to own his property with."

The judge also turned to Kurt, who'd learned by then to look back at his elders as if they were equals.

"If he did," Chris said, "I'd go along with it. I'd immediately agree to have my name taken off the deed and the bank accounts. But still. He's only eighteen. He's a bit young, I'd say, to be making a lifelong commitment to another person."

Kurt openly laughed at the absurdity of that argument.

"I don't intend to do anything else in my life," Kurt said to the judge as he pointed his finger at Chris, "without that man by my side to help me. You can call him my best friend, my brother or whatever else you please, but that's the way it is."

Kurt hadn't bothered to wait for his turn on the witness stand to make his remarks.

The judge asked the clerk to swear in Kurt as a witness. After the clerk did so, the judge asked the court reporter to repeat Kurt's remarks.

When the court reporter was finished, the judge turned to Kurt again.

"Do you wish," he inquired, "for those words to be your testimony in this case?"

"Yes, I do," Kurt replied. "That's what I want."

Neither the judge nor Kurt had chosen to consult Kurt's shoulder-shrugging attorney.

The judge looked at Gwendolyn. "I'll hold you responsible if anything goes wrong."

Gwendolyn laughed. "Nothing, Your Honor, could make me happier than being responsible for Kurt and Chris. I'm quite certain we're doing the right thing here."

Kurt had used the Boeckers, among others, in his argument with

Chris and Gwendolyn.

"Edna had Karl on her deed," Kurt had said. "Aunt Juergen had her friend's name on her deed. Arny told me he'd put Elaine on his share of any property he might come into. My grandmother Bertha was on the deed to every property and bank account my grandfather owned."

Kurt got his way. The judge signed the order. Kurt and Chris jointly owned the farm.

The judge also ordered that Kurt could remove the Kensington State Bank's claim against his grandfather's estate based upon Henry's cosigning for the loan the bank had made to Chris and his father. Kurt did it by paying off the loan.

*****

After a celebratory lunch with Aunt Juergen and Gwendolyn at Rodney and Tim's, Kurt and Chris returned to Mount Reinhart.

The oaks and hickories in the woods were in full red-and-yellow October bloom.

When Kurt and Chris reached the top of the hill, they paused and looked back at the creek valley where the story they'd fallen into had begun a half century ago. Without becoming pillars of salt, they felt the comfort of the other man's arms.

"Reader," Kurt whispered, quoting the nineteenth century line he and Chris loved, "I married him."

Author's Note

If you enjoyed reading this novel, I would very much appreciate your leaving a review of it with the online bookstore where you bought it.